Acclaim for David Martin Anderson's

THE LAST GOOD HORSE

"One of the best stories ever written on the exploitation of our mustang herds. David Martin Anderson weaves a gripping and emotional tale of murder and betrayal in Montana."

— *G. Ray Field, Director, Wild Horse Foundation*

"David Martin Anderson's compelling novel takes the lid off nostalgic illusions about wild mustangs being part of the 'Proud Heritage' of the American West. Anderson reveals a depth of human brutality and greed, and places before us a crisis of conscience over the violence towards horses, slaughter, and profiteering that continues today. 'The Last Good Horse' takes us out of our comfort zone and demands that we look squarely at our mercenary past. . . . and reminds us of the forgiveness, beauty, selfless service and grace granted to us throughout history by the horses."

— *Alicia Nation, President, NM Mustang & Burro Association*

"An absolutely brilliant tale. . . . one of the first to tell it the way it really happened."

— *Albert Botha, President, Save the Mustang Foundation*

THE LAST
GOOD
HORSE

By
David Martin Anderson

ConRoca Publishing

ConRoca Publishing
132 Ridge Trail
Boerne, TX 78006
210.485.6764

Visit our website at
http://www.conrocapublishing.com

or the author's website at
http://www.TheLastGoodHorse.com

Also, visit the author interview on YouTube at
http://www.youtube.com/watch?v=7gwaP6-ZT-w

ISBN 978-1-892617-16-3 (Paperback)
ISBN 978-1-892617-17-0 (Digital)

Printed in the United States of America - March 1, 2011

Originally published as a paperback edition in May, 2010 as an 'Advance Copy'
 for promotional distribution only

10 9 8 7 6 5 4 3 2 1

For Papa

Foreword and Acknowledgements

To say this novel is primarily about the demise of the American mustang would be misleading. While it is true that one of the story's central themes entails the systematic killing off of our horse populations during the 1930s, the plot, itself, digs far deeper and, some would contend, far darker than just the issue with the mustangs. At its core, this story is about human tragedy, one that happens to parallel that of the horses. It is a tale about one man's search (Billy Bartell) for meaning and inner peace during an epoch coming of age period (1939) in American history. In a very real way, seventeen-year-old Billy Bartell represents that America—inexperienced and innocent to a world about to embark on a journey through hell. Perhaps that is why I cast him as a wandering-but-lost soul, much in the same vein as Dante in his search for heaven.

Likewise, one has to wonder what sort of people in 1939 would have allowed the mass slaughter of such a majestic and innocent creature as the mustang. After all, those same animals helped Americans settle the West, helped plow farmlands, deliver mail, provide basic transportation, and transform the nation into greatness. Horses were truly that generation's friends and allies. Sadly, however, from 1914 to 1939, over four million mustangs were rounded up and processed into chicken feed and dog food in what became known as 'the great removal.' Less than one hundred thousand mustangs remained alive by the end of that pivotal year.

It was while reading an article in *National Geographic* on the subject that it struck me (like a ton of bricks) how, in the mad rush to mechanize everything, our country turned its back on the wild mustang herds. The truth is in 1939, *no one cared* about the slaughter that was taking place. Thus, I felt compelled to journey to the source of what has become today a contentious battle between our Federal government (i.e., Bureau of Land Management) and the protectors of the last great herd on Pryor Mountain in Montana. The fruit of that journey is this story.

I would like to acknowledge a number of people that helped me in this undertaking and for whom I am grateful for their assistance: Arnie Shreffler, Frank Anderson, David Law, George Clayton Anderson, 'Cowboy' Larry Bonnville, Peter Riva, Ed White, Claudia Law, Knoxie Edmonson, R.G. Anderson, and Mike & Candy Hagan. Lastly, I want to express my gratitude to my wife, Mary, for making the journey to Montana with me. Throughout the years, she has made these wanderlusts of mine truly memorable. Thank-you, everyone.

"God forbid that I should go to any heaven where there are no horses."
    - R. B. Cunningham-Graham, 1917 letter to Theodore Roosevelt

I

I tried my best not to kill any of 'em. Problem is when you worked for the rendering company you sorta got used to all the killing going on. Then it comes easy.

Don't much like to think about that previous life. For seventy years I did my best to block it out. Seventy years is a long time to try and forget. Had a lotta trouble sleeping cuzza what I did. When I could sleep the bad dreams would come to haunt. So you can imagine how I felt when I opened my eyes and saw the woman sitting next to my hospital bed. She had no clue I'd be coming back around. How could she? I'd been pronounced dead thirty minutes earlier and she was facing the door blowing cigarette smoke into an empty hallway.

"If you don't mind, I'll take one of those smokes," I said to the woman. And with that the poor thing jumped to her feet and dropped her cigarette on the sheet covering me up. Nearly set me ablaze. Stammered and stuttered and kept repeating herself while hunting for that lit butt. Asked me if I knew I'd been pronounced dead. Even asked me if I wanted the priest back in the room.

"No, Ma'am. A smoke is all I want. Far as getting that priest. Probably not a good idea. I gave up on organized religion a long time ago."

"But I don't understand what's happening," she kept saying. "You were dead. Clearly dead. I saw it with my own two eyes. Now you look as healthy as a—"

"Horse?"

"Yes," she said. "And a sound horse at that."

I told her I didn't understand what was happening neither but here I was about to get in one last smoke on the devil's dime. "You are that woman I sent for, ain't you? The one that rescued all them mustangs down in Nevada?"

"Yes, I am," she replied. "And I drove over eight hundred miles to get here but you were unconscious by the time I arrived."

I couldn't let that one slip by. "Well then, guess it's a good thing I got a pass from dying or you would have come all the way for nothing."

"Now-now, Mister Bartell," she said. "I really didn't have a choice in the matter. Did I? They told me you wouldn't tell the priest anything about the horses or what made you do the violent things you did at Potrero Gap."

"That's right, Ma'am. Just kept my mouth shut the past seventy years. Nobody was gonna listen to my side of things, anyways. And that priest sure as heck wasn't gonna do me any favors. You see, I wasn't a very good man back then."

I guess those words must have torn the woman up some cuz she gave me one of those you-poor-wretch smiles and then sat back down in the chair and handed me a cigarette. And I'm sure I looked pretty miserable. Like I could kick off again at the snap of the fingers. Maybe that's why she got so eager to hear what I had to say.

"Well, here I am, Mister Bartell. At your service. And please don't call me Ma'am. Call me Annie. Okay?"

"Okay, Annie. Long as you call me Billy." And with those words exchanged I didn't waste anymore time. Death might fiddle a body a second verse. Lung cancer won't. "Truth is, Annie, you're the only person who can stop the mustang roundups still going on here in Montana. If you can stop 'em in Nevada then you can stop 'em here, too. So, I figured if you knew about the bad things that went on at Potrero Gap, you could get President Obama to put an end to it. What went on at Potrero ain't right. What went on down there no creature, two or four-legged, should ever have to endure. Sabe?" She nodded her head she understood and I scooted up higher in the bed and pointed to the door. "If you

don't mind shutting that. Best we not let on to anyone about my rebound."

Annie reached past the end of the bed and closed the door so the night nurse couldn't hear our voices. She turned back to me and spoke in a whisper. *"I'm fully aware of your part in the killings that went on seventy years ago, Billy. I'm aware of more than you may know."*

"I understand," I said. *"But there's more to it than meets the eye."*

"Oh? And how's that?" she asked.

"Well, for starters you need to know that I never took pleasure in it. But I was just seventeen at the time and angry as all get-out. And I made some bad choices. Really bad choices."

"Fine, Billy," she said. *"I'll try to remember that and remain impartial and listen to your side of it, if that'll ease your conscience. But there's only one thing I can really offer you."*

"And what's that, Annie?"

"To try and save your Montana mustangs," she answered.

"If you can do that," I said, *"that'll sure give me some peace of mind."*

And peace of mind is what I needed.

2
(1932)

There were moments in the boy's life that made him the human being he would later become. Whether the moments had been set in motion as part of some grand scheme or the boy freely chose his destiny within life's random chaos remained unclear until death. What is clear is when the boy's fate changed, so did the fate of the horses.

Snow fell on the hunters as they slept. The last heat remaining from their smoldering campfire radiated tepid from a massive boulder the two huddled against. The man woke up first. He shivered watching the fire's smoke ebb in a lazy plume and assumed the late-March storm now fronted miles away. *Or did it?* He rolled over to gaze up at the sky and watched as morning blackness faded to pale indigo. Venus flashed on the horizon to the northeast but no stars glimmered overhead. Instead, high wispy cirrus clouds stretched out of the south as faint glints of red from the sun's first rays etched their trailing edges. Reading these signs, the man reasoned the front had indeed passed and the day's weather would be favorable. He also guessed the time to be 6:30AM and knew they needed to get moving. He and the boy had a full day ahead.

With a sense of uneasiness, the man stretched his frozen arms and legs. He unbuttoned the flap on his bedroll, shook off the snow, and slipped on his boots. He crawled to what remained of the fire hoping to revive it but no embers ignited from his clumsy efforts. Frustrated, he slid the iced-over coffee pot to the side and decided to gather kindling. The day's first light played tricks with his equilibrium as he searched for wood and he stumbled. When he fell for a third time, this time to his knees, he wondered why he hadn't stayed put in the warmth of the bedroll. When he struggled to get up something caught the corner of his eye and he turned to watch the horses stir spooked. He limped to where the three mares corralled in a makeshift pen and checked the tie downs and draw straps. Everything appeared in order. He punched through a layer of ice in the canvas buckets so the horses could draw water. As a precaution, he scanned the area outside the rope pen, but nothing moved or seemed out of sorts. Again, he felt dizzy so he knelt on a knee. When he looked back toward the boulder, the boy still lay inside the other bedroll with the head cover drawn tight against the cold. The boy was snoring.

This child is no hunter, the man told himself. Still, he couldn't help but eke out a pensive smile reminiscing the day his father took him hunting, there at Stratford Mountain. During that outing he had managed to shoot a jackrabbit. Well, it was more like a starved and lame bunny, far from the monumental trophy kill a father could imagine for a son in Bighorn country. Then again, his own boy was a mere ten years old, three years younger than he had been on that first hunt. He knew better than to expect miracles from a ten-year-old. And the more he thought on these things, the more he reminded himself how this hunt had a much deeper implication. This outing was about passing along a family tradition. It was about bonding between father and son and making memories that would last a lifetime. Mostly, at least from his perspective, it was about spending quality time with the boy while he still had the chance.

He drew a deep sigh and then tried distracting himself by peering northeast to the trailing clouds and toward his home in Billings. Even from twenty miles away, he could make out the town's lights. The sun still hung low enough on the horizon that the opaque halo would last another minute or two before red and then pink and then orange washed over it. Watching this sunrise he realized few remained. The thought left him feeling melancholy and he swallowed hard to keep from tearing up. The boy doesn't need to know I'm dying, he kept telling himself. All the boy needs to know is that I love him.

He tiptoed back to the campfire and lit some tinder and small branches, and stoked the flames with his breath. A few minutes later, the fire blazed and he set the coffee pot back in its center. He threw in a handful of coffee grounds and while the brew heated up went to relieve himself behind the boulder. When he returned, he shook the boy out of a deep sleep. "Wake up. Wake up, Billy," he whispered. "There's something wonderful I want you to see."

The boy poked his head out of the bedroll with his eyes gunked shut. The man wet his thumbs with his own saliva and then, wiped the caked eyelids open and kissed his son on the forehead.

"Come on, Billy. Up and at 'em. You've got to see this."

The boy moaned as he yawned. He pawed for his cowboy boots at the bottom of the bedroll and slid them over his iced toes. He shivered outside the warmth of the bed and did little to help himself get dressed. He struggled to fasten the red Pendleton hand-me-down, but with his father's warmer hands, the winter coat buttoned with ease. By the time the last button hitched, the boy had become distracted blowing steamy breath high in the air and watching it disappear in a swirl. His father ignored the shenanigans and concentrated on cinching up the drawstring to the oversized Montana cowboy hat.

"There, Billy," he said. "Even old Tom Mix would be proud of you."

The boy slurped some coffee to warm up, but the man refused to let him finish and nudged him to get going. "We haven't got all day," he said. "Now bring along that new birthday rifle. You never know. Just might come in handy."

The boy seldom questioned his father and snatched the rifle that had been stashed inside the bedroll. The .30-06 bolt-action Winchester Model 54 had been a father-to-son gift. Many considered the newest deer rifle made by Winchester the most accurate ever manufactured. When the boy's father turned thirteen, the boy's grandfather started a family tradition by gifting a Winchester Model 1894. "That's why I gave your brother a rifle six years ago and why I'm giving you this one now," his father had said. "It's a Bartell tradition. Hopefully, someday you'll do the same for your son."

They hiked to the far side of the boulder and slid down a short path to a toppled fir. The massive tree had recently fallen; enough greenery remained to conceal them as they peeked through its limbs. The man pointed at something in the distance and the boy squinted to see the object through the dim morning light. At first, the boy had trouble believing his eyes, so he blinked and blinked again until the thing came into focus.

"*It's a wild mustang,*" the boy stated. "Biggest, whitest horse I've ever seen."

"I'd venture to say it's over sixteen hands. Probably came up south from Pryor Mountain."

The horse had climbed out of a brushy thicket and now stood stiff-legged and motionless on a large rock with its front half exposed to the first rays of the sun. Even as father and son continued to watch, the white of the stallion's chest and shoulders began to capture flashes of red. The boy whispered to his father how the red looked like the bull's eye red on some of the targets back at the shooting range.

"This ain't the shooting range, Billy. This is the real thing. What we came here for."

"But, Pa, it's a mustang. We don't shoot mustangs."

"The heck we don't. Government pays ten dollars for mustang ears."

"But, Pa—"

"No buts, Billy. If you're gonna take the shot, you'd better hurry up."

The boy tossed some pine needles in the air and watched the tailings settle straight down. He knew the wind would be less of a factor than the drop. With the horse positioned upwind at least a thousand feet, he would have to adjust the aperture two clicks up.

"You may be right, Pa, about hurrying and such, but I think we oughtta wait."

"And why's that?"

"I need more light."

"*Light?* That mustang is a perfect shot right now. Shoot while you can."

"Pa, that mustang ain't going anywhere. He's waiting on the sun to warm him up."

The man thought the boy's logic sound and decided it best to let him have his way. "Well, you're the boss. At least make sure your safety is on until you're ready to fire. Okay?"

The boy drew an exasperated face. "Of course it's on, Pa. Cowboy commandment number one says 'a Cowboy should always be safe with his gun' and that's exactly what I do."

The words tickled the man and he held back making a full belly laugh. He pinched the boy's nose and told him how much he, too, liked Gene Autry's cowboy codes. Being a father, however, meant following paternal codes like asking sons obvious but foolish questions.

While they waited for more daylight, the man turned around to check on the horses. Even from the lower perspective, the animals appeared spooked and he was at loss to understand why. Maybe the mustang got the horses riled. Maybe it was just the cold or overnight hunger pangs. Only after the lead mare resumed pawing the snow for food did he feel a sense of relief and leaned back against the tree trunk to ponder the boy. To be able to shoot a wild mustang and make money seemed a stroke of good luck. Could it be that the boy was a natural-born hunter after all? Had he misjudged the lad's baser instincts to kill? The boy certainly knew how to handle a rifle—one of the best shots he had ever seen.

"Pa?"

"Yes, Billy."

"Do you think they'll ever find Mister Lindbergh's baby? The one that got kidnapped?"

Given the setting, the man found the timing of the question odd and he frowned. "Why do you ask that? *Now*?"

"Well, Pa, it just bothers me. That's all." The boy took his eyes off the target to watch his father's face. "I just can't imagine what it'd be like for Mister Lindbergh to lose his little boy. I mean, whoever took him away from his pops did a bad thing. Taking a baby like that, maybe killing him for money, that ain't right."

"No, it ain't right, Billy. Killing one of God's children for money never is."

The boy nodded his head in agreement and then turned back to eye the mustang. Resting the rifle on the tree trunk, he took a practice aim. Even from a thousand feet the white horse seemed extraordinarily beautiful. The boy continued talking while aligning the sight aperture.

"Pa?"

"Yes, Billy."

"Isn't a horse one of God's children?"

"It ain't the same. I was talking about people, not horses."

"Seems the same to me, Pa."

"And I'm telling you it ain't."

"Well then, if it ain't the same, I don't believe in God."

"Billy, don't you ever say that again. The devil will swoop you up if you aren't careful about what you say. Got it?"

"Yes, sir."

"Then, hush up."

The boy nodded his head and then began wiping down the muzzle of his rifle barrel, frowning over his father's sternness. The silence lasted all of fifteen seconds.

"Pa, did you ever take Ma hunting when she was alive?"

"No."

"Why not?"

"Cuz your Ma got queasy. She never liked dressing out dead critters. Made her sick to her stomach."

"Well, I guess I'm like Ma cuz I don't like cleaning dead things, neither."

"Well, you need to get used to it, Billy. How else are you gonna help your brother run the Bartell funeral home someday?"

"Henry can run it just fine without me."

"Look. I built the business so you both can make a living if something were—" He stopped mid-sentence. It occurred to him that his son's unusual chattiness could be a stall tactic. "You don't want to take the shot, do you?"

"I'm thinking on it."

"Billy, what's there to think on? A trophy like this one may never come again."

"I know, Pa. *But it is a horse.*"

"We already talked about this." The man shook his head in frustration. He thought for a few seconds over how best to coax the boy into shooting. Maybe the boy misunderstood the true importance of the day. "Look, Billy, you'd make me real proud putting down that wild mustang. Real proud."

"But you always say a person should shoot what he plans to eat. I don't plan on eating horse meat."

"This is different, Billy. This one's a trophy. You don't have to eat trophies. We'll sell his ears and I'll cut off his mane and you can hang it in your bedroom and every time you look at it, it'll remind—"

"I don't like looking at horse scalps, Pa. I'm a cowboy, not an Indian. And I don't wantta cut off its ears, neither. Cowboy commandment number four says 'a cowboy is always kind to children, old folks and animals.' Killing that white mustang ain't being kind to animals."

"Look, Billy, it's your mustang to kill or not. At that distance, you'd be darned lucky to put it down, anyways. So, do what you wantta do. I'm just gonna sit here and look the other way. You make the call. Just do one thing for me if you decide to pull the trigger."

"I know, Pa. I know. *Always aim straight and true. Never rush the moment. When you're finished, savor what you've done.*"

The boy watched his father's eyes dart away from his own. He watched as his father pretended to be gazing to the rear toward the mares when, in fact, the man's pursed lips and swiveling jaw said all that needed to be said. Hesitant to take the shot, the boy decided to go through the motions and placate his father, but ever so slowly. Maybe the mustang would dart away or move out of range while he stalled for more time. With this strategy in mind, he planted his arm on the tree trunk to steady the rifle and, like his father, pretended. He pretended to work the aperture sight and peep down the barrel. He made painful faces as if the aim, itself, strained his eyes. To make the playacting look even more authentic, he released the safety. Yet, as he sighted in the mustang's shoulder, he noticed movement fifty feet below the intended target. A mountain lion had crept out of the brush and crouched ready to attack. A few seconds later, it sprung forward and leaped in the air. The boy pulled the trigger.

The man said nothing until the boy appeared satisfied with the shot and had set the rifle snug against the tree. "Good boy, Billy. How'd you do?"

"Killed it, Pa."

"Well, that wasn't so hard now, was it?"

"No, Pa. Not one bit."

3
(SEVEN YEARS LATER - 1939)

"What's the count, Chief?"

Hayyel, also known as 'the Chief,' kept his eyes fixed on the herd while swiping the air behind his back. Sully ignored the hand signal.

"Chrissake, Chief. Leastways, gimme a guesstimate." Sully pressed.

The Indian scout belly-scooted six inches lower on the boulder in case the lead mare detected his partner's voice or saw the sun's muted reflection off his ten-power French stereo binoculars. His boot toes dug tight into the boulder to keep from sliding all the way down. Again, he propped his elbows wide and splay-like to steady the binoculars. Then, he resumed the count in a loud enough manner so Sully could hear.

"One-twenty-one. One-twenty-two. One-twenty-three. . . ."

From a thousand yards away, the herd spread out in a tight protective circle high in a valley above a seasonal watering hole. Weeks-old foals romped behind their mothers while two wise old mares directed the herd in a slow but methodical gait to the crest of a hill where morning sunlight would wash them in warmth. Near the hill's crest, a sea of blue columbine and pink bitterroot waved through a meadow of clover. Halfway down the hill, where shadows stretched horizontal, meadow grasses clashed green against pearl-colored snow with the snow losing the battle to a fresh June breeze. Even farther down, the trailing edges of the snow turned translucent and snaked into the watering hole that drank its icy runoff. En route from the Bighorn River basin to Pryor Mountain, the mustangs had not passed this way since seven summers before. Now cultivated with a cornucopia of edible greenery, the place overpowered the herd's sense of survival brought on by a long sterile winter. Today hunger cast aside caution.

As the two mares nickered commands, the other horses, especially the yearlings, ignored them. Nourishment had been hard to come by for months. Now they refueled by gorging on the crawl. The true lead mare strutted from the rear, weaving in and out of stubborn yearlings while nudging them onward.

The second-in-command mare, a red dun with three white socks, served as assistant and steered the pack from the front. Hers was an honorary role in a caste order eons old. The position coveted her as matriarch without equal. She was the oldest broodmare of the lot, yet had been barren the past three years. She had also had her good years replenishing the ranks and doing what nature required for the herd's survival. Now, at age sixteen, the next few months would prove to be her last. Already her teeth had ground flat from gnawing on juniper and sage at the lower elevations during winter. Unable to digest soft grasses, colic or malnutrition would spell her demise. Nevertheless, she moved on with the herd, oblivious to her own predictable end. Her priority now was tending the two-week old foal that had been following her everywhere and suffered from separation anxiety after losing its mother to a pack of wolves.

Even as Hayyel scouted these sights, his count continued unmoved by the majestic beauty of the valley or the rarity of the herd's breed, or what he knew would be in store for the horses by the end of the day. ". . . One-forty-eight. One-forty-nine. One–fifty. . ." When he glassed the herd's vanguard, he noted the tireless red dun with three white socks that commanded the herd's respect. He watched as a white palomino foal nuzzled the matriarch for milk and as the dun nipped the foal but just as quickly groomed the youngster's withers and mane while the foal's tail wagged. Though the sight of the dun and the foal caused him to break a tentative smile, the feeling lasted for just a second or two. Then, he resumed the count.

He scanned farther down the slope past the laggards and the true lead mare and the old buffalo wallows left centuries before, and readjusted his aperture to focus on the distant watering hole where the boss stallion, a brown roan, lay soaking. It was a rare sight for a boss not to be lurking in the shadows and watching over his harem while protecting them from prey or other stallions. This particular boss, however, had let his guard down savoring the herd's good fortune, and he lacked the experience to protect them from the greatest predator of all—man.

"Well, dang it all Chief. What we got?" This time Sully pressed the question loud enough that one of the broodmare's ears perked forward.

Hayyel turned around and placed a finger over his mouth before muttering, "*Hush*. We have Spanish jennets. The ones from seven years ago."

That stirred Sully's interest more. His voice rose to a shrill. "You're telling me we finally out-foxed Old White?"

Perhaps there was nothing Hayyel could say to keep Sully from blowing their cover. Conveying the white man's word 'hush' meant nothing to the animated Texan. Not learning English until the age of twelve put the Crow scout at a unique disadvantage. Stumbling for the right expression, his mind conjured 'shut up' or 'pipe down,' or would those expressions offend his cowboy friend? The fact remained every word he attempted to translate took time and Sully stewed impatient. English, that is Texas-styled English, never made sense. Exasperated, Hayyel replied slowly and deliberately, in the manner he always spoke. "*No*. Old White, he has moved on. We have a new boss. A brown roan. And you must speak with a soft tongue or we will lose the herd."

"So what's the numbers?" Sully whispered.

"One hundred sixty-three with five foals. All livestock, they look sound. All look winter thin. Most have stripes on their backs and withers. Full-sized Spaniards is what we have."

Sully started dancing a jig. He giggled and slapped his hat hard against his jean legs.

"What are you doing?" Hayyel asked, this time perturbed.

"You don't recognize my Indian whoop-it-up dance, Chief?"

"*No*."

"Too bad. Just try not to spoil the moment cuz right now I'm happier than FDR on a Saturday night."

"And why is that?"

"Cuz these Spanish mustangs outweigh those pintsized ponies we caught three weeks ago. Scrawny as these here might be, we're gonna get rich off 'em. *EeeHaa.*"

Hayyel ignored his partner's antics. He slid down the boulder, snatched the signal flag off the packhorse and climbed to an outcrop. From his new vantage, he glassed the other side of the valley to a location a mile away. He could make out Lieutenant Mullin and Toothless Bob through the thin morning haze standing on a cliff in front of towering two-hundred-year-old Douglas firs and staring in his direction. From their position, a steep incline tilted down three hundred feet to the valley floor. The herd lay in between with the horses sauntering to the west toward the crest of the high meadow. Potrero Gap hunkered thirty-five hundred feet below and ten miles southwest. And through it all—Sully's antics and his exposure on the outcrop—the herd had remained oblivious to human presence. This would be an easy roundup, he told himself. It would be the closest any herd had ever come to the company's stockyard in the twenty years he had been doing this— all within a half-day's ride of the gap. It meant the crew would be dressing out and rendering the horses that night and for the next forty-eight hours non-stop. It also meant he would be climbing Bopwadesh Hill under a full moon and a clear night sky to perform the ritual. This is a good omen, he told himself. "*Máwalipé biyuhpadkia,*" he whispered to the rising sun. Then, he waved the signal flag high in the air and checked to see if Lieutenant Mullin saw it. The next movement he spied through the binoculars was Mullin releasing Judas and the black stallion charging down the incline toward the herd.

4

Nine miles to the west another horse hoofed down an incline—*to die.* The Crow people called the aged stallion 'Remliel' (translation: one who awakens the soul) but the cowboys and old-timers knew the elusive creature by a less complex name, 'Old White.' To the Indians the white palomino symbolized the wandering spirits of the 'ancient ones,' the founders of the Crow nation; to them Remliel was most sacred and holy. The cowboys, on the other hand, summarily cursed the wily stallion for outsmarting their traps and defying their barbed wire fences; to them the horse was nothing more than a herd-stealing nuisance. Both cultures, however, agreed on one point: the horse had lived on Pryor Mountain through multiple generations of man. Only a handful knew the truth. Hayyel was one. To debunk the legend, he often told his people how he witnessed the stallion's birth in 1922. He told them how a year later he attempted, and failed, to round it up as a renegade colt. "What it means," he tried explaining, "is that Remliel is just like the other mustangs, only smarter. Then again," he would typically add, "any horse that survives the wind and the cold and the white man's slaughters for that long deserves praise."

Seventeen years of existence is an eternity by feral horse standards. Most never see ten. Remliel's longevity traced to his ability to learn through observation and apply the acquired knowledge to survival techniques. All wild horses learn in this manner to some degree but, like humans, there are those that learn from their own mistakes and those that learn from the mistakes of others. The problem for mustangs is that making too many mistakes, either way, lead to premature death. White men often refer to the mistake-free horse as possessing 'horse sense' (or horse intelligence). The Crow Indians call it '*izaquabak*' which, loosely translated, means cunning-sly.

Survival for Remliel entailed mastering the art of warfare. His ability to size-up an opponent, to assess the foe's vulnerability and use the acquired information to defeat the foe in battle paralleled the same tactical thinking used by samurai warriors. And it kept him alive.

Once Remliel turned four he began challenging for herd supremacy. Most six and seven-year-old bachelor stallions lack the mental maturity to challenge the herd's boss. Not Remliel. He watched how other herd bosses fought off challengers. He learned from their victories and their defeats. When the day came to overthrow the lead stallion, *his father*, he caught the foe off-guard and chest-butted him into a deep ravine.

During the next twelve years, other herd bosses and overconfident bachelors challenged Remliel hoping to usurp his reign. Some of the combat waged for hours. The long scar running from his withers to his right elbow testified to the three-hour clash with a young grulla determined to steal his harem. The more youthful grulla eventually boxed him in a canyon where it attacked with its sharp hooves, shredding Remliel's coat and opening a one-inch-deep gash. When the grulla reared a third time, Remliel head-butted it to the ground and then viciously stomped it to death. The fact the challenges never let up is why Remliel eventually wore down. When the brown roan, *his son*, challenged him and won, Remliel abdicated his throne and took up residence in the rear echelon with the young stallions.

Then the day came when Remliel wandered off to the west. Instinct guided him on an appointment with death to the top of a remote hillside that lay far from the security of the great meadow. There, he stood looking down upon rare aspens, a small field, and a gaped washout protected by an endless cliff. Below the cliff, a barren mesa towered and buildings sprung from the parched earth surrounding its base. He had never laid eyes upon manmade objects: stockades and reefer boxcars and a tin roof bunkhouse. He had no idea what Potrero Gap stood for or its purpose. Yet, standing on the hillside, he felt no fear. If anything, he felt curiosity.

As he moved toward the aspens, he watched horse manes dancing magically in the wind. The manes dangled from leather strands laced to the aspens' lower limbs and numbered by the thousands. Swirled by the breeze, the manes brushed against his shoulders as he strolled in and out of the trees, working his way down the hill. When he breached the tree line where the small field began, he knew his wanderlust had ended. From that lookout he would stay and smell the aroma of the clover and take in the strange new sights below. He would bask in sunlight, watching day ebb into night, and then close his eyes content to know he had once been a great king.

5

When Judas reached the herd he had a ten-minute head start on the cowboys. It meant he would have to fend for himself longer than normal. His master and the company proprietor, Captain Belial, planned for such contingencies. The Captain invested years in training the prize stallion on how to dominate a herd and defeat foes in battle. Herd domination, however, was just one piece to the rigorous training puzzle. Once Judas defeated a boss in battle, the deceiver would shepherd his naive flock back to Potrero Gap while the drovers pushed the herd from behind. The methodology always worked. In a sense, the tactic fostered a symbiotic relationship between Judas and the cowboys; each needed the other for successful roundups. Judas provided the false sense of leadership while the cowboys provided the fear that kept the horses moving forward.

When the black stallion found no boss to engage in battle, he attempted to draw out the foe as trained. He circled the herd shaking his head, whinnying insults and bucking his hind legs in a showy display of bravado. Even with the larking about no boss emerged. Undaunted, he high-step cantered through the herd's center and straight to the lead mare, wearing a brassy swagger while shrieking in staccato squeals: *I am Judas. I am a mighty warrior. Where is your leader? I have come to challenge him.* Again, there was no response. Now furious, he charged past the rear vanguard bumping bachelors, trampling foals and knocking down yearlings. He stomped his feet and used the best of his old tricks to mesmerize and manipulate. Judas-the-Great, he proclaimed, now reigned as their new leader.

Eventually, the brown roan heard the commotion and stirred to life from the lazy soak in the watering hole. He galloped up the steep incline shrieking in protest. Judas commanded the higher ground and lay in wait. As the two horses tussled for position, the black horse drew first blood, hoofing the roan in the head. Stunned, the roan fell back before charging again, this time taking a biting gash out of Judas' neck. With blood pouring out, the roan bit again in the same spot. The third charge caught Judas off guard and the black horse slipped and fell. As the boss reared to stomp, a rifle shot cracked and the roan collapsed to the ground in a thunderous wallop.

All four cowboys galloped to where the roan lay dead. They pulled back hard on their reins and skidded to a slick grassy halt. Sully spoke first, hollering to his partner. "Nice shot, Toothless. Looks like we'll have to start calling you *One-Shot* from now on." He grinned ear-to-ear and spat a chaw of tobacco on the dead roan. "Didn't know you and Mister Winchester were capable of such dastardly feats from a hundred yards and on the run."

Bob smiled wide exposing the four-tooth gap on his uppers. "Hell, Sully, from a hundred yards I even look purdy."

"Indeed, you do."

Lieutenant Mullin seemed more preoccupied with the herd scattering than in Judas moaning and bleeding to death. He galloped forward to head off any potential losses.

Hayyel dismounted to check on Judas. "This looks bad. I will need to cauterize the wound. Sully, you bring me the butane burner off the packhorse. Bob, you go catch up with Lieutenant Mullin."

Judas rolled on his side and lay in a state of shock. Blood seeped from the gash.

"Damn it all, Chief. Bad enough Judas got mangled, but if he dies Captain Belial will kill us all." Hayyel nodded his head in agreement and scowled at the thought. "Well, then, you'd better fix him fast and fix him good," Sully added.

Within a few minutes, Hayyel had a poker fired red-hot. Sully had his entire body weighing down Judas' head and his hand pressed tight against the wound. He gave the go-ahead and Hayyel plunged the iron tip inside the gash. Steam shot in the air followed by the stench of burning horseflesh and a long hideous hiss. Judas screamed out in pain and tried to stand up but Sully held on, riding the horse's neck. Hayyel kept the poker in the wound longer, and

Sully capitulated to the fury by covering his ears to keep from hearing the horse's agony. When Hayyel gave the okay, Sully jumped off. Judas stood and shook. A faint hiss still sizzled where the poker had plunged, but the fix seemed to hold.

"Never heard a horse scream like that before," Sully remarked, showing some rare empathy.

The words ignited something dark inside Hayyel and he stepped to within inches of Sully's face, lowering his voice to an angry rasp. "Oh, no? How about all those mustangs in the kill chute? You never heard them scream when the bullet misses its mark? When you botch a kill?"

Sully disliked Hayyel's tone and fired back. "First off, Chief, the new bell gun fixed all that. No more misses. No more screamin'. Second, you're the one that kills 'em. You're the one that slits their throats and bleeds 'em out and hollers Indian mumbo-jumbo. So, don't you give me any a that holier than thou malarkey just cuz your conscience is catchin' up."

Hayyel stared down Sully but then stepped back. He knew Sully's rebuttal made sense—a rarity for Sully. The truth was after slaughtering horses for twenty years, his conscience had, indeed, been bothering him. He turned around without saying anything and walked away swiping the air behind his back. Maybe this time Sully understood the hand signal.

6

While the sun hid behind Pryor Mountain, Captain Leonard Belial shuffled toward the camp's front entrance, dragging the mangled leg that had plagued him for twenty-one years. His destination, the company mailbox, still lay over a hundred yards farther ahead. Halfway down the steep caliche road, a sound caught his attention. He paused to listen as an out-of-sync windmill gear screeched in pain and made a mental note to have Sully grease its gears. Then, he continued along the road, having for an instant forgotten the urgency of the hurried pace.

With the crew rounding up horses on the mountain, 'the Captain' was forced into retrieving his own dispatch. The fact he had worked up the courage to abandon the 'big house' stood as a testament to his overt fixation for the daily newspaper. After all, he had never quite accepted the newfangled radio Lieutenant Mullin installed years earlier. Newsprint still satisfied his voracious appetite to stay connected to the outside world.

Even now, protected by the long shadow of the mountain, the filtered sunlight played havoc with his light-sensitive eyes. He knew that in a matter of minutes the sun would peek above the crest and blind his retreat. He despised sunlight and cringed at the realization he waited too long to begin this tedious excursion. His pace quickened. As he stumbled along the road, he wondered how in the world he had ever forgotten the welder's glasses and the wide-brimmed hat still sitting on the credenza. The thought worked up to a self-loathing lather and he burst aloud with an earsplitting curse that scared off a covey of quail pecking at grout. Even the quail knew better than to get in Captain Belial's way.

Just the morning before, his cowboys had left camp to chase after the last of the wild herds. Like previous roundups, he could only guess as to when they'd return. Thus, until the moment they rode triumphant through the gap, he would pass the time in the solitude of his study by maintaining a vigilant watch. Until they returned, he would fend for himself. This particular morning, a fresh newspaper and a new bottle of brandy would share the vigil as he listened to one of Mozart's melodic string concertos on the old Victrola. No doubt the news might be a few days old, but time meant little at Potrero Gap while sipping fine brandy.

Once the mailbox unlatched, he began separating letters from the menagerie of post and came upon the weekly issue of *Life* magazine. The cover photo caught his attention—the Statue of Liberty aglow at night. He couldn't help but notice how beautiful 'The Lady' looked in the photo, and managed to cast a rare smile as a thought struck. "Both of us, dear lady," he purred, "look much better in the dark." The words smacked of self-deprecation. The Lady, indeed, looked majestic, lit up by a camera's flash. He did not. The facial disfigurements he suffered during the war had grown so grotesque that he seldom allowed himself to be seen by anyone. Likewise, it had been fifteen years since his last visit to town. That disastrous outing had frightened a group of schoolchildren into a bawling fit.

Now, with the sun about to strike his face, he tucked the mail under an arm and began the retreat. He flipped through the magazine while tackling the uphill ascent. Absorbed by the latest news-in-photo, the harsher sunlight seemed less offensive to his eyes. And as he scanned through the pages, he discovered himself staring at a picture—two Canadian corpsmen standing next to their small reconnaissance aircraft. The aircraft looked like one of the newer classes of private civilian airplanes. One of the men was pointing to a location on a map while the other eyed where his comrade pointed. The man pointing appeared to be a pilot. The other, a ground crewman, shouldered a newly designed radio communications backpack. The staged photo instantly churned gears inside the Captain's head. His retreat grinded to a halt next to the windmill where he stood agape in wonder over the possibility of these newest twentieth century marvels working in tandem. Then, as that idea struck, the sun washed over his face and he screeched in pain. His voice echoed off the walls of the gap and up toward the mountain.

"Gotcha. . . *Gotcha.* . . *Gotcha.* . . . "

7

By 3:00PM the contingent of mustangs and cowboys had pushed below Sage Creek and down the hillside funneling into Potrero Gap. Judas had rallied from near death, and was leading the procession to the stockades and the awaiting slaughterman. The black stallion never once shirked from his duty or, for that matter, gave any indication he had bled out eight hours earlier. In fact, once he caught sight of the stable, his pace picked up to a brisk canter. The herd's pace quickened as well.

The cowboys had formed a tight semi-circle to the rear and sides of the mustangs with Hayyel to the left and Lieutenant Mullin on the right. Both men jockeyed along their respective flanks to insure strays didn't wander too far away. Sully and Bob brought up the rear whistling and shouting the herd forward. Sully cracked his whip every now and then, mostly for Bob's amusement. Each time the whip cracked, one of the foals would whinny or whimper and a mare neigh in disapproval.

Potrero Gap ended less than a tenth of a mile from the camp facilities. From that point onward, timber fencing crisscrossed the company's grounds. The vastness of the stockades attested to the days when Pryor Mountain roundups brought in two hundred horses every week. Lately, roundups were lucky to bring in a hundred horses every three weeks. Besides the endless rows of fences, the camp embraced a rickety barn housing a vintage 1920s electric generator, a dilapidated stable and paddock built out of rotted and chinked pinion logs, a washed-out plank bunk house devoid of paint, a company supervisor's house (also known as the 'big house'), culling chutes, overhead hoists for conveying carcasses, a windmill needing grease and a terminus railhead where iced-down milk cars (reefer cars) waited ready for the next shipment.

The big house sat on higher ground than the rest of the facilities and commanded a view of the pens, the abandoned fields in the valley and the approach down the hillside into the gap. On a clear day, Captain Belial would spy a herd drawing near and play a welcoming tune on his spring-wound Victrola record player, amplifying the sound over an old PA speaker. Today's selection was a Boston Symphony version of Mahler's *The Adagietto*.

Anyone or anything descending the mountain had to pass through the gap. There was no other way off or on the mountain. The foothills from the mountain broke into an endless line of cliffs that straddled a fault line. The sheer rock face served as a castle wall, keeping the mountain range impenetrable from the west, south and east. The cliffs also kept the horses safe from man. What changed everything was the great Pryor flood of 1909. The flood washed out sediment underneath the hill leading from Sage Creek. The washout created a draw or gap a quarter-mile long. Wide at the upper elevation, the fissure narrowed to less than sixty feet at the bottom. From that point onward, the land opened to the flats where manmade railing took over the task of funneling herds the short distance to the stockades.

On the northeast side of the camp, a mesa rose four hundred feet and sloped to the south where its shallowest incline (its 'bench') intersected the railing and the gap. The mesa, known locally as Black Mesa, served as a landmark as in, "Where 'bouts you boys holed up?" Answer: "Why, right b'low Black Mesa where the gap washout took place."

Beyond the camp, broken down windmills dotted the barren landscape where farmer after farmer tried scratching out a living, sod busting for wheat. The abandoned farms were a legacy from the dust bowl storms of 1933 to 1935. This stark contrast between the arid flats and the lush mountain explained why some folks claimed Potrero Gap stood "smack dab between heaven and hell."

Bob and Sully heard the music as soon as they rode out of the gap and into the flats.

"What in tarnation is the Captain playing this time?" Bob took off his hat out of respect for the music. "Don't you know nothin', Sully? It's from an opera. It's a dirge called *The Adagietto*. The Captain, bein' the kind decent fellow he is, knows these mustangs are gonna face the executioner tonight. He's doin' it outta respect. You do know that this is one of Mahler's masterpieces?"

"No, I did not. Awful kind of the big boss," Sully replied, impressed. He thought it over a bit longer and then squinted one-eye suspicious at his partner. "Say. What in hell is a *dirge*? And just how in the world do you know all that?"

"Simple. I am a supporter of the fine arts. And—"

"*And what*?"

"And Captain Belial had me pick up that record for him last time we was in Laurel. The Lieutenant filled me in on everything. Gave me a right smart education on the music, he did."

Sully laughed and swiped the air at Bob with his hat even though Bob rode twenty feet away. "You almost had me, Compadre."

"Indeed." Bob smirked.

Sully pushed up a yearling that straggled off and then swung his horse around. "Say, what you gonna do with your cut of the money from this bunch?"

"Buy my little girl back in Texas a dress I seen in town. It's a copycat of one Shirley Temple wore. Pretty and frilly and full of little pink polka dots." Bob's eyes welled up. "She's such a Daddy's girl."

Sully grinned knowing the setup about to come next. "That may not be such a good idea, to buy her that dress, that is."

"And just why not?"

"Cuz she's eighteen years old, Bob. Eighteen-year-olds don't wantta look like Shirley Temple. They wantta look like Judy Garland. They wantta wear nylon stockings and push-em-up bras and drink martinis sophisticated-like. Why at eighteen—"

Before Sully could finish his tease, Lieutenant Mullin turned back and hollered out, "Time to cull out the foals, you two."

It meant that Sully and Bob were supposed to separate the babies from their mothers. No money could be made off malnourished foals, so once the herd cleared the gap and began the short run to the pens, separating out the foals became standard operating procedure. Culling meant shooing the foals back up the gap while pushing the mares forward.

Without hesitation, Sully cracked his whip but none of the foals budged. He cracked the whip a second time, directing his energy at the youngest of the lot, a white palomino colt. The tip of the whip slashed the youngster's back, drawing blood. The foal screamed out in pain. *Bad mistake.* The surrogate mother, the red dun with three white socks, got involved. She twirled around and chest-bumped Sully's horse. Sully grabbed hold of his saddle horn to keep from getting jarred off. The other broodmares reversed direction to follow the lead of their matriarch.

Lieutenant Mullin watched everything unfold. "What's happening back there?"

"They won't budge. Broodmares 'bout to revolt. Should we bring the foals into the pens? Separate 'em in there?"

"No. Keep 'em the hell out."

"Then what you want us to do?"

"Shoot 'em. Shoot 'em where they stand."

Bob pulled out his Winchester rifle. He took aim at one of the foals.

"You ain't gonna shoot that baby, are you Bob?" Sully positioned himself in front of the foal.

"Indeed, I am"

"What for? Don't do nobody no good to kill a baby."

"The hell it don't, Sully. Puts food on the table and buys Shirley Temple dresses."

"For Chrissake, Bob, this one's just a week old. Let it go."

"Nope. Now move aside."

Sully punched Bob in the shoulder. "Damn it all, Bob. You do everything the Lieutenant tells you to do? Mullin says jump and you jump. Mullin says kill and you kill. You a company man? Is that it?"

Bob sat up straight. He scowled at Sully, thumbing his chest. "You better believe I'm a company man. One hundred percent guaranteed I am, and don't you ever forget it. And so are you." He spun his horse with his back to the herd. "You know why we're here, Sully, and what's in store for our kind if we don't make good on the pact we made down in Texas. Now move the hell aside."

Sully backed his horse and Bob fired a bullet into the head of a foal. Three more shots fired and three more foals dropped in the dust. Bob side-kicked his horse closer to the week-old white colt and placed the barrel muzzle flat against its head. "You're the little hellion that started all this," he yelled at it.

From out of nowhere, the red dun charged full-speed blindsiding him. Rider and horse tumbled against the railing, busting out the weathered slats in the fall. Bob rolled to safety behind the next fencerow. Just as he rolled, the dun scrambled through the opening and charged up the caliche sloped bench leading to the top of Black Mesa. The other horses followed her, as did the white foal. All struggled in the ascent. All dashed in spurts, spraying loose gravel and dust in the air as the grade began wearing them down. Sully rushed to his partner's aid. Bob was dazed but quickly climbed back on his horse. Meanwhile, half the herd had escaped up the mesa before Lieutenant Mullin and Hayyel could cut off the rest.

"You two go after that bunch and bring 'em back down," the Lieutenant shouted. "Hayyel and I'll drive this group in the pens then come back to help you. Think you can do that without screwing it up?"

"Yes, sir," they both replied.

Sully dismounted and took hold of his horse's reins. He walked the horse to where the bench to the mesa began.

"What are you doin', slowpoke?" Bob complained.

"Tell you what I'm doin'. I'm walkin' my horse up. No way he's gonna climb tiptop with me onboard. Not on that steep a grade he ain't."

Bob dismounted, too.

8

Just below the aspen tree line, the white horse watched everything unfold. He watched as seventy horses clawed their way to the top of the barren mesa to flee from predators. He watched as the two-legged creatures scaled the crest in pursuit and blocked the herd's escape route, the bench. When at last he recognized the red dun, a sense of dread overtook him. *This was his herd.* The dun had birthed seven of his foals; the yearlings and others all bore his distinctive markings.

Frantic, he bolted down the hillside, through the small field and to the cliff's edge for a better view. Now, from a thousand feet away, his tail shot vertical from a rush of adrenalin. He snorted and pawed the ground, for there was nothing he could do but watch from afar. The predicament defied his most basic instinct to protect. He paced along the precipice and whickered across the gorge. When the horses heard him, they reacted by stampeding in a broad circle along the mesa's drop-off looking for a way to escape. There was none. Out of desperation, he shrieked to his family: *Save yourselves. Save yourselves.*

9

It took Bob and Sully four times as long as the mustangs to ascend the mesa's bench. Once on top, Sully doubled over gasping for air. "I ain't as young as I used to be," he whined.

"Tell you one thing, Compadre," Bob wheezed, "if we don't wrestle this wild bunch back down, you won't be getting any older. Captain Belial will make damn sure of that."

"Alright, One-Shot Bob, got any smart ideas on how we go 'bout doin' it?"

Bob scanned the mesa's topside but focused his attention beyond the herd to the east and the white horse off in the distance. "Looky over yonder." His head nudged toward the far cliff.

"I'll be. Is that Old White kickin' up this tempest?"

Bob grabbed for the Winchester. "Won't be kickin' much longer. Kill the king and win the battle, I always say." He took aim and fired a shot. The white horse stood his ground, statuesque, without flinching. Bob fired a second and third shot with the same results.

"Hey there, *Three-Shot*. Believe you need to engage the tang if you wantta hit the target."

Bob flipped up the tang sight on the rifle. He knelt on one knee to steady his aim and then squeezed the trigger. The shot missed. Sully had already broken out the binoculars and attempted to serve as spotter.

"That one went ten feet at ten-o'clock."

Bob fired again.

"Fifteen feet at four-o'clock. Say, I wonder, *Five Shot*, if we parked a barn over yonder if you could hit its broadside?"

Bob threw down his hat and stomped on it. "Tell you one damned thing, Sully, I may not be good at a thousand feet, but me and this rifle can knock down anything that moves at less than three hundred and that's without the tang." To prove the point he flipped the tang back down, took an iron-sight aim at the week-old white foal and dropped it with a perfect shoulder shot.

The kill spooked the herd even more. All seventy horses raced west and looped along the mesa's perimeter in a futile scramble. They stampeded past the two cowboys, kicking up a cloud of silt that swept skyward in a violent dust devil swirl. Led by the red dun, the herd circled again and again. After minutes of desperation, the mustangs leaped off the mesa reaching out to their old leader. One by one, they tumbled down Black Mesa to their deaths, never once hesitant in their decision.

Sully spat some chaw and stared at the dead horses piled up at the bottom. "Damnation. Never seen nothin' like that before."

"Me neither."

"We got a lot of cleanin' up to do, you and me."

"Indeed."

"Captain gonna be madder than hell."

"No doubt about it."

A few seconds later Bob cupped his ear and craned his neck to hear something faint from off in the distance. "Listen," he said.

Sully grimaced straining his ears. "I'll be. I hear it. It's *The Adagietto*."

"Indeed."

For the next five minutes, both men stood mesmerized on top of the mesa soaking up the melodic sound of Mahler's dirge as they stared at the dead mustangs.

Sully spun to look at Bob. His face beamed. "Guess what? Looks like you're One-Shot Bob, again."

"Oh? And how's that, Compadre?"

"Cuz that one shot of yours just put down over seventy mustangs."

Bob thought over his new nickname. He smiled wide and toothless. He liked it. He liked it a lot.

10

"So, what you gonna do tonight, Squirt? Go to the picture show?"

The boy ignored his brother to focus on lowering the last of three cadavers into a casket. The three deceased—an old man, his wife and granddaughter—mangled beyond recognition from a car wreck outside of Billings the day before. The last body belonged to the eighty-seven-year-old man. The man's face contorted, all but sheared in half with the right side remaining intact. The man's corpse would be the only one of the three viewable. The boy turned the man's head toward the coffin's sidewall, fluffed up purple satin liner to hide the disfigured half and brushed makeup on the good side. He stepped back to admire his work. "That oughtta do it, Henry," the boy whispered.

Henry peered over his brother's shoulder. "You sure did a nice job mending him. His kin are gonna be real happy to see him one last time."

The boy mulled over the compliment and let loose with an overdue sigh. Between the all-night vigil prepping the three cadavers and his recent expulsion from high school, he had yet to decide which of the two calamities caused him to feel more nauseous. One thing, for certain, *Henry would be furious over the expulsion once he found out.*

Still eyeing the deceased, the boy couldn't help but ponder his own relevancy in a world that indiscriminately altered lives. "Henry, do you think he was a good man?" he asked.

"I'm sure he was. From what I hear, half the town will be showing up at this afternoon's wake. His son told me he worked for the railroad years ago. Ran the entire Montana region. Must of been some big shot."

The boy nodded his head, accepting the notion that with so many people showing up for a funeral, the man had to have been 'good.' Yet, the idea of why a person so good could die so tragically never made sense. The boy had seen scores of similar tragic deaths over the previous seven years. Few made sense. "So what's the point?" the boy burst.

"The point, Squirt?"

"Yeah. He lived a good life. He died for no reason. And nothing changed. The world goes on like he never even existed. *So, what's the point?*"

Henry struck a serious pose. He placed his hand on his brother's shoulder. "That man's reward for being good in this life is eternity in the next. That's the point." He paused to make sure he had the boy's attention. "It's still not too late to get baptized."

Before the boy could respond with his customary '*it ain't gonna happen,*' the doorbell rang. He brushed away his brother's hand and sprinted up the basement staircase two steps at a time, still wearing his blood-spattered apron and rubber gloves. "Hey, Squirt. We need to finish our talk," Henry hollered after him. The boy, however, raced too preoccupied to respond and darted for the front door. He had been expecting the Western Union agent. Even now, recollecting the conversation from the night before, the telephone call seemed more like a dream. The voice on the other end of the phone said a telegram formalizing the offer would arrive before noon. Sure enough, when the boy swung open the door an agent stood at attention with an envelope in-hand.

"Billy Bartell?" the agent asked.

"Yes, sir. That's me."

"I have a telegram for y—"

The boy snatched the envelope and slammed the door. He bound up the next flight of stairs leading to his bedroom, tore open the envelope and read the slip of paper. Everything appeared word-for-word as he and the mystery man discussed. Pleased, the boy let out a squeal and tossed the gloves and apron to the floor. He reached underneath his bed and dragged out the duffle bag packed twelve hours earlier, and snagged the Montana cowboy hat off the dresser. Before leaving, he manhandled the sheathed rifle from behind the door, threw it over a shoulder and stumbled down the stairs, dropping the gear by the front door.

"Henry," he yelled into the basement. "We need to finish that talk. *Now*."

11

Sully and Bob worked the next twenty hours nonstop, dragging mustang carcasses back to the rendering yard *by themselves*. Sully's prediction about Captain Belial being madder than hell had been all too accurate. In fact, the other cowboys had been forbidden to assist the two screw-ups in the backbreaking task, not that Hayyel and Lieutenant Mullin desired to work all night in the cold.

Despite the sub-fifty degrees nighttime temperature, the salvage operation became a hurried rush against rigor mortis and rotting horsemeat. The company's '36 Ford AA flatbed tackled the repetitive loop around the rocky backside of Black Mesa amazingly well. Without the truck's ramp and hoist and overhead lights, Sully and Bob could not have accomplished the job. Just three mustangs mangled beyond salvage and Sully made the managerial decision to "leave 'em to the buzzards." The other sixty-six were hauled on the flatbed two at a time, thirty-three roundtrips in total.

After the last carcass was dressed out and rendered, the cowboys took a four-hour breather. All four men wanted a break from the afternoon heat before tackling the remaining ninety head of livestock, the ones still alive in the pens. With a meal under their belts, they would be rejuvenated and in better shape to labor until finished.

Years earlier, Captain Belial had installed floodlights to facilitate working round-the-clock. Some of the cowboys preferred laboring at night when temperatures dipped into the forties and fifties. Cooler temperatures also improved crew efficiency—up to two more processed horses per hour. Cooler weather had the opposite effect on captured mustangs. Typically, a herd would become riled trying to stay warm. This seemed even truer of the

Spanish jennets. They had gone without food and water for thirty-six hours and had nothing to burn to generate heat. They sensed something afoul. Moreover, with half their herd missing, the red dun vanished and their once great leader, the brown roan, dead, they had every reason to be jittery.

By midnight, with the last of the herd rendered and carcasses hung in the reefer cars, Bob and Sully sat on the kill chute railing, exhausted from the work and chilled by the night air. Sully's attention span had shifted to a well-deserved night off in Laurel on Saturday, the next day. "I aim to pump up the local economy," he bragged.

"Oh? And how's that, Compadre?"

"The regular way: women and alcohol."

Bob was preparing a comeback when the glow from the full moon played tricks with his vision and he held up his hand to block the light. He blinked blindly, glancing up at the lunar orb radiating from behind Black Mesa. Silhouetted against the moon, the white horse perched in perfect stillness. It had been watching the cowboys slaughter the last of the herd.

"My. My. My. Looky who the cat drug back," Bob remarked.

Sully turned around and almost fell off the railing. "I'll be. Old White don't give up, do he?"

"Nope."

"You gonna take a shot?"

"Nope."

"Why the hell not?"

"Cuz the Captain hired us a real marksman to do the job. Some kid outta Billings named Billy Bartell. He'll be here tomorrow."

12

The moon had risen overhead by the time Hayyel stumbled to the top of Bopwadesh Hill. Judging from the position of both the moon and the stars, he guessed it to be after 3:00AM. He also guessed he had fallen behind schedule. The two heavy-laden satchels had slowed his ascent. The horse manes, all one hundred fifty-six of them, needed hung before sunrise.

When he reached the aspen tree line, he discarded the satchels and spread out a worn Indian rug. Lit up by the moon's luminescence, the multi-colored rug radiated traditional Crow powder blues and greens, both colors interwoven into an eight-point star. The rug had belonged to his great-grandfather.

He abandoned his clothes and sat naked on the rug, cross-legged and facing what would be the moon's westward trajectory. When he gazed up at the sky again, the infinite grandeur of the stars and constellations overwhelmed his senses. For a brief moment, he wanted to forget how he was losing this battle against time and that he wanted to relax and soak up the splendor of the night. But he couldn't. Too many souls depended upon his work. The ritual, this ritual, always took priority. He let loose with a moan of capitulation, wondering if he could keep doing it—sacrificing horses—or if what he was doing at Bopwadesh Hill made any sense in the greater scheme of things. Twenty years of performing the same rite had changed nothing. The killings still kept on. Soon there would be no horses left on the mountain. And just how many spirit horses did the ancestors need? He wondered. Old doubts started to resurface and he knew better than to dwell on such things. In the end, it will work out, he told himself. *He-That-Hears-All* has a plan.

He took his hunting knife out of its sheath and cut off a strand of his own shoulder-length hair. He raised the knife high in the air

with his right hand and raised the strand in his left, and then prayed
aloud beseeching the Crow giver of life and death:

> "My name is Hayyel Gabriel and I am a human
> being. I am the proud shaman son of Runs-With-
> Deer, daughter of the Crow Nation. I am the proud
> shaman son of Winston Gabriel, Yankee son of the
> city of New York and Federal Agent to the Crow
> people. I bleed Crow. I bleed Yankee. I bow to no
> man. I bow only to He-That-Hears-All."

When he paused to collect his thoughts, a shooting star fell from
the sky. Convinced this was a good omen, he continued:

> "This Crow country is good country. He-That-
> Hears-All has put it exactly in the right place.
> Everything good on this earth is to be found here.
> Everything here is bountiful and endless. That is
> why tonight I once again can bring you more spirit
> horses. . . ."

Eventually, his prayer become a melodic chant to the god he
worshiped. He began to sing in his native tongue about the great
hunt of two days earlier and about the capture of the wild
mustangs. He sang about the horses' bravery in death and about
their goodness and innocence and purity. He sang, asking that the
spirits of the noble mustangs be gathered and taken to his ancestors
so that the mighty Crow warriors of old could ride the horses they
loved on earth once again on the hunting grounds of heaven.

When he finished his beseeching, he stood and thanked his god
for listening. Then, he began the solemn task of tying the manes to
thin leather strands and suspending them below the limbs of the
aspens, all before the sun would rise and the stars and the moon
would vanish.

XIII

First time I ever saw a cadaver laid out at our funeral home was a month after my Pa died. The year was nineteen thirty-two. Henry came running into my bedroom in the middle of the night and commenced to shake the sleep outta me. "Get up, Squirt," he says. "I need your help." I remember rolling over in bed wanting to go back to sleep and him getting madder than hell and tossing me down the stairs. Wasn't too pleasant an experience. Now up to that point I'd never set foot in our morgue. Place scared the you-know-what outta me. Of course Henry knew this. He knew the only way he was ever gonna get my ornery hide to help him was by force. That night Henry succeeded.

In those days a family funeral home was just that. Your living room got turned into a parlor. The dining room became a place for wakes. And your basement got turned into a morgue. In a town the size of Billings there were only two undertaker families. Both come into the business cuzza parent learned the trade and passed it onto the kids. The good news for me was while I grew up around it my Pa had spared me the gruesome details until he thought I'd be old enough to handle it. Let me tell you something. At age ten I wasn't old enough. Pa knew that. Henry didn't.

So getting back to that night—Henry shoves me into the basement and as I come into the morgue I look up and see this woman lying naked on the slab. Couldn't of been more than nineteen years old. Henry had already laid her out and gotten her prepped and ready for embalming. Mind you. I was a short scrapper and that table stood about as tall as me. Looking up at that woman all I could see was her profile. And what I saw was a woman who looked more alive than dead. She was pretty as all get out. And did I mention she was pregnant? Eight months pregnant she was. Her belly was swollen up and her breasts all droopy-like and bloated. So I turned to Henry and I remember saying, "She doesn't look dead." And him saying she was fresh cuz her old man had just shot her four hours earlier. The man got himself drunk. Said he didn't wantta baby. Guess he got his wish.

Anyways. I couldn't believe it cuz from my angle she looked normal. So I grabbed a stool and stood on it to get a better looksee. What I saw was a small hole in the woman's forehead no bigger than my pinkie. The woman's eyes had been closed shut and I figured it was all right to poke my finger in the hole to see if it was real. It was. And Henry starts laughing and shaking his head. "What's so darned funny?" I asked. And Henry comes back and tells me that for someone scared of coming within a hundred feet of the morgue I was taking to it like a duck to water. I ignored him and kept checking things out. "What's this?" I remember asking while pointing out a slug on the table. He told me he'd removed the thing from her brain. Turns out the Sheriff was gonna use it as evidence to hang the man. I said, "Then what do you need me for?" And he said, "To take out the baby. They want a separate burial for it."

Before I could say or ask anything else Henry takes a scalpel and un-zippers that poor woman. Defiles her body. Cuts her clean from the sternum to the pubic bone. Runs the knife three more times through layers of skin tissue and muscle all the way through the placenta. I was in too much shock to run or scream. All I could do was stare. Then he pulls apart these things he just cut on and there curled up inside the woman is this baby boy. Dead.

With Henry stretching the woman wide open he looked over at me and says, "You lift the baby out and I'll cut the cord." I knew better than to argue again else suffer the consequences. So I reached in and lifted the boy up. Couldn't of weighed more than four pounds. "He's still warm," I said. "What'd you expect?" he says back. Then he got real serious and real angry at the same time. Not with me but with the whole situation. "I knew her, Billy," he says. "She went to school with me. I really liked her a lot. She'd *come to school with bruises and cuts and whatnot. Had a bad home life. One day I walked her home. Carried her books. When we got to her house her pa saw her with me. Got madder than hell cuz she was with a boy. We was only thirteen. Innocent as it gets. But her pa was crazy jealous and he threatens me and slaps her and grabs her by the arm and drags her inside the house with her screaming the entire way. I should have killed him then and there. I coulda saved two lives. But I made the wrong choice."*

All of a sudden Henry gets all choked up. I'd never seen him before or since shed tears like that. And he looks me square in the eyes and says, "That son-of-a-bitch raped her. Her own pa. Let me tell you something, Billy. If you don't remember anything else in life, remember this: There's good people and bad people in this world. The good ones deserve to live. The bad ones deserve to die."

And he's telling me all this while I got the baby in my hands. And I'm thinking to myself how much that baby deserved to live. And how easy it would of been for Henry to have changed all the events leading up to that night if he'd just outright killed the man. Now I'm not saying Henry blew it or nothing like that. What I'm saying is that sometimes killing a human being to spare a life is the right thing to do. Killing can be a good thing. At least that's what I believe.

So when Henry was done saying what he needed to say he told me to put the baby in the sink and wash <u>it</u> off. Now that upset me and I said something like, "<u>It</u> is a boy. And as of now <u>it</u> has a name." Henry went along with what I was driving at. "So, what's the name you come up with, Billy?" he asked. And I said "Isaac" on account Pa's name was Isaac. Henry liked my giving the baby Pa's name.

As I look back on those years it doesn't take much to figure out why I wanted to get the hell outta Billings first chance come along and become a cowboy. Washing off dead babies in a sink. That sorta work wernt ever for me. When I finally turned seventeen and left I shoulda just hopped the first train come along. Shoulda rode the rails and took off for California. Going to Potrero Gap. . . guess that was my wrong choice.

14

The two-mile hike from the main rail line to the camp's railhead should have taken forty-five minutes, but the heat, the flies and the weighty combination of the duffle bag and rifle slowed the boy down. Over an hour late by the time he staggered to the front gate, he felt relief by the sight of the fir log entrance. The Π-shaped entrance bore a hang-down sign with the camp letters 'PMRC' (Pryor Mountain Rendering Company). Higher up a buzzard sat on the massive cross support. The boy had failed to notice the bird before. Now startled, the gangly buzzard seemed threatened by his presence. It hissed and cawed at him. The boy found its behavior odd since most buzzards scatter anytime humans get within fifty yards. He bent down to pick up a rock to peg the bird, but as he straightened up a small inscription penciled on one of the vertical timbers caught his eye. He dropped the rock and his duffle bag, laid down the sheathed rifle and walked over to read the handwritten message. Someone had scribbled the inscription five feet off the ground on the stripped-bark portion of the fir beam. The writing smeared and the boy blew dust away for a better look:

> Abandon hope all ye who enter here.
> Dante Alegre – '33

"You must be the kid the Captain sent the telegram to."

The voice caught the boy off guard and he jumped back startled.

"Sorry to spook you like that. The name is Sully. Sully Beatrice. Glad to meet you." Sully held out his hand and clamped down on the boy's.

"Billy Bartell. Glad to meet you, too, sir." The boy nodded to the inscription. "Say. Who's Dante Alegre?"

Sully shrugged his shoulders and lied straight-faced. "Him? Shoot, he was one of the young drovers hired on a few years back. Didn't like it here. Just disappeared. Gone in a flash. Didn't even collect his pay." Without elaborating, Sully manhandled the duffle bag over his shoulder and handed the rifle to the boy. He eyed the leather rifle sheath, changing the subject. "So, kid, what you packin' inside the leather? A model ninety four?"

"No, sir. It's a fifty four, thirty-ought-six with a nineteen thirty-eight Beeman aperture sight."

Sully whistled impressed. "Is that so?"

"Yes, sir."

"Well, now, ain't you quite the shot? Heard you won the open shootout upstate last summer."

"No, sir. That ain't correct. I won the under twenty-one tri-state championship."

Sully slapped his thigh and giggled. "If that don't beat all. Wait until Bob hears about this."

The two walked up the drive to the bunkhouse. Along the way, Sully pointed out the camp facilities and yakked non-stop, mostly about how the cowboys had earned a much-deserved Saturday night off and that they were taking the Ford flatbed to Laurel that evening. The kid could tag along if he was so inclined.

When they entered the bunkhouse Bob and Hayyel were preoccupied playing cards and smoking pipes. The room reeked of stale cherry tobacco. An older-style RCA radio cabinet propped in a corner with a windup alarm clock sitting on top. Background music played from the radio. The boy thought he recognized Bing Crosby's voice and assumed it to be from the afternoon broadcast out of Billings. The room had been swept clean and the creaky floorboards looked as though someone had wet-mopped the aged planks just for the new hired hand. The two single-hung front windows opened to the empty stockyard but the smoke from the pipes had yet to escape and hung eye-level and caustic. Six bunk beds sat on one side of the room in two neat rows; four of the beds had all eight feather mattresses coiled up tight against headboards gathering dust. Two sets of beds were prepped, square-cornered and tucked in clean with brightly colored wool blankets. The other side of the room housed a crude kitchen with worn porcelain cabinets and an enormous pine table that could seat fourteen. A vase with a rose sat in the center of the table. At one end, Hayyel sat relaxed with a boot propped on top, teetering back in his chair, with a stack of multi-colored poker chips piled chest high. Bob's heap of three white chips pales by comparison. A third chair turned open with cards facedown and void of chips.

"A bunch of no-good cheats they are," Sully teased.

Upon hearing Sully's slander, both Bob and Hayyel stood up and shook the boy's hand. Sully gave out introductions.

"This here is the Chief, least ways that's what we call him on count he lives on the Crow reservation eight months out of the year. Keeps to himself most of the time until there's a card game come up. Then, he gets real friendly-like and takes your money. Thinks he's real smart cuzza the education he got on the reservation. My advice to you is to stay away from the Chief, especially after he's been drinkin' whiskey. He'll start spouting Robert Burns or Elizabeth Barrett Browning."

"Or worse," Bob threw out. "He'll read that stuff to you when you're trying to sleep."

Hayyel just shook his head and sat back down realizing he would never get a word in. Bob remained standing and felt compelled to speak up before Sully stole the entire show.

"Bob Virgil is the name. Some call me Toothless Bob—"

"On count he lost his front teeth in a saloon scrape down Texas-way," Sully chimed in.

"That's right," Bob said, "But you shoulda seen the other cowboys." As he said the words his partner, Sully, threw out a 'that-ain't-right-look' and Bob corrected himself. "Actually, there was just this one cowboy."

"And he was short. Real short."

"Yup. I cannot tell a lie. He was short, all right and kinda old. But I did best him, especially once he knocked out my teeth." Bob paused as if recalling the night of the scrape. He scowled with the recollection. "Kid. Why don't you just call me One-Shot as a professional courtesy. I'd prefer it." He winked at Sully. "So, did my Compadre warn you about his cooking? About his beans? Did he tell you that the upper bunk ain't the place to hang your hat with him underneath?"

Sully took off his hat and swiped it at Bob. "You are a poor excuse of a man."

"Indeed, I am."

Even Hayyel caught himself laughing aloud. "Say, One-Shot, once I take those last three chips from you," he asked, "will you wager the penny?"

Sully spoke up. "Nope. Cuz it ain't his no more to wager."

Bob swivel-turned to face the boy. "Kid, are you not sporting a model ninety-four?"

"No, sir. It's a fifty-four."

"With a modified dual tang?"

"No, sir. It's a—"

"Beeman aperture just like I said," Sully finished. He reached into Bob's shirt pocket and snatched the penny. "And the kid won the under-twenty-one tri-state also just like I said. Looks like you're buying poontang tonight at Miss Edna's."

Puzzled, the boy looked from man to man. "*Poontang?*"

Hayyel explained. "Our two Texans bet on anything that strikes their fancy. Usually they wager an old Indian-head penny. Bob told Sully he heard you won the open in Helena and Sully said that was not right and they argued themselves into a fistfight."

Sully interrupted. "That penny usually keeps us from scrappin', that is, most a the time. That's why we wager it. Just lost our heads a little. That's all." He spat chaw onto the floorboards and wiped down his mouth after checking the sore swivel to his jaw.

"And the Chief come up with a new idea to help keep us on the straight and narrow," Bob added. "He says every time we get worked up into a physical tercation—"

"Altercation." Hayyel corrected.

"—altercation, and that it should cost us both dearly and monterly—"

"Monetarily."

"—to make us think twice."

"Like a police fine," Sully broke in.

"That-a-way we'll think twice 'fore gettin' in another fistfight."

"And our big money wager was that the loser had to buy poontang for everyone up at Miss Edna's place."

"Guess that means you're getting free poontang tonight, seein' as how you're now one of us," Bob added.

Sully whispered in a not so soft manner, "*Us* as in non-management."

"Non-management?" the boy asked.

"Us peon workers. Not Lieutenant Mullin or Captain Belial. They live in the big house. They ain't like us," Sully stated, a little too self-assured.

"I think they're queer for each other," Bob added matter-of-factly.

Hayyel laughed. "You are two crazy white men. Truth is, boy, the Captain owns the PMRC and Lieutenant Mullin is the foreman. They live together. They have history. They fought in the Great War together. The Captain, he suffers from a mustard gas explosion. His eyes are sensitive to light. He does not leave the big house and uses Mullin to relay his orders."

"I've seen the Captain once," Bob spouted.

"You don't wantta see him twice. That's for damn sure," Sully offered. "He's ugly as the devil."

"Smells somethin' foul."

"Blackest eyes I ever seen."

Hayyel started laughing again. "You two are going to scare the boy especially since he must go talk with the Captain in a few minutes." Hayyel looked at the clock sitting on top of the radio cabinet. "And I think he is late."

"Well, I ain't takin' him up to the big house," Sully stated. "I did what we agreed to. I met the kid down by the entrance. Your turn, Toothless."

Bob swallowed hard. "I don't like this. I'm not the one who drew the short straw. Tain't fair."

Sully shook his head as if in pain and handed the penny back to Bob. "There, Compadre. Does that help?"

Bob looked at the penny and rolled it in his fingers. "I take back everything back I ever said about you. You are a good man."

Sully beamed. "Indeed."

15

After knocking on the door, Bob made a quick beeline back down the hill, mumbling over his shoulder how the boy was now on his own. Once he disappeared, a voice from inside and toward the rear of the house hollered to come inside. The boy pried opened the door and peeked from around its edge. "Where are you, sir?" he asked, hollering back.

"Follow your instincts, son. Come down the hallway."

The boy stepped in and patted the door shut. Black curtains had been drawn over the windows to protect the Captain's light sensitive eyes. Whatever light did filter through muted in twilight gray and kept the interior in a state of uneasy limbo. A pale light bulb flickered in a back room, what the boy assumed to be a study, and he followed its dim glow down the corridor.

The hallway was papered ceiling to floor in old newspapers, except for an exposed bead board section near the study's entrance. Most of the newsprint had yellowed in varying degrees and spanned a period of twenty years. All of it was front-page news and most bore *New York Times* publication stamps. The headlines spoke to a variety of notorious or well-publicized murders: the 'Kansas City Massacre,' the 'Wineville Chicken Murders,' 'The St. Valentine Massacre,' 'Leopold and Loeb' et cetera. But one of the headlines—the Lindbergh Baby Murder—caught the boy's eyes and caused him to stop along the way.

"Hardly any space left is there, son?" The voice bellowed. "I'm waiting for just the right headline to finish it off. Twenty years in the making."

"Captain Belial is that you?"

"Mister Bartell, I presume?"

"Yes, sir."

"Come. Sit. As you have already observed I possess an inquisitive fascination into human nature and to the age-old question of what motivates man to kill? I hope that doesn't upset you."

"No, sir."

"It is quite the paradox, Mister Bartell, isn't it? In spite of the great achievements of this twentieth century of ours, civilized man continues to murder. Have we learned nothing? Are we no better off, no more ethical than our ancestors in their primordial caves? And what is to come next? Another world war?" The voice paused. "Please. Please step inside and have a seat so I can see you. We have much to discuss, you and I."

The boy felt his way to a worn Victorian couch and sat. He took off his Montana cowboy hat and fumbled with its brim while checking out the study. The air inside the room smelled musty-old and hinted of something familiar. The morgue had smelled like it the time he and Henry embalmed the defrocked priest who had committed suicide. Or was it the drifter who got gunned down after killing the family at Fry? He couldn't remember which. Maybe the smell was just a coincidence. The air, however, chilled dank like the basement back at Billings. The thoughts caused him to feel an onset of nausea. He stretched his neck and popped it attempting to distract himself from the queasiness. Through it all, he sensed the captain's eyes staring at him from behind the desk like a mountain lion preparing to pounce. Even earlier when the voice spoke, it didn't really speak. It purred. Now veiled by a purple scarf shrouding the lampshade, the faceless shadow seemed to be stalking him. He held up a hand to block the lamp's glow but still could not make out the mysterious figure.

"It's quite all right if you don't see me. An old war injury has disfigured my face and eyes. I'm afraid you might find it terribly distracting." Captain Belial hesitated long enough to lean forward in his chair and fold his hands together on the desktop. They shook in a Parkinson's-like palsy; liver spots dotted pale white knuckles and wrists. "So, I trust you had no problem finding me?"

The boy vacillated before answering, unsure if the Captain meant the camp or the big house itself. With the question, he detected a hint of an accent, which in the hallway seemed British in origin. It was at that moment, as he paused to respond, that he wondered what would bring someone from such a faraway place like England to the isolation of Potrero Gap. Then, to avoid the awkwardness of silence, he answered, assuming the Captain meant finding the camp, not the big house. "No, sir. Just followed the directions you gave in that telegram."

"Good. And I trust you got introduced to the crew and got settled in at the bunkhouse?"

"Yes, sir. I met them all."

"Excellent. I would introduce you to the fifth member of our merry band, Lieutenant Mullin, but he is on an errand for me in Denver. You will meet him upon his return on Monday morning. So, do you plan on partaking in the crew's camaraderie this evening in town?"

"Yes, sir. I plan on going."

"Good. Now, would you care for a cigarette before we get down to brass tacks?"

"No, thank you. I don't smoke."

The Captain thrust an entire pack at the boy. "Trust me, son. Before you finish the job I propose, you'll become a smoker. Keep the pack."

The boy reached across the desk, took the cigarettes and stashed the pack in his shirt pocket for no apparent reason other than not to appear rude.

"So, that brings us to the reason why I invited you here to work for me. First, let me digress." The Captain leaned forward even more, exposing his mouth and chin to the pale light. "Believe it or not, I have been quite anxious to meet you ever since you shot that mountain lion and made the front-page news of the *Billings Star* seven years ago. You see, Mister Bartell, you have a rare skill. A rare one, indeed. I read with delight how, as you grew older, you began winning riflery tournaments around the state. I watched as you became a marksman without equal. Your accomplishments in such a brief period of time are nothing short of remarkable. You should be commended for all the hard-working endeavors you undertook that led to your proficiency. Likewise, I am aware of those tragic aspects of your personal life: your mother passing away when you were four years old, followed by the death of your father when you were ten. I know that your brother raised you and that you learned the honorable trade of an undertaker at a tender and impressionable age. I know you despised that sort of work. And I would be the first to acknowledge that children should never be exposed to death in such large doses. Death should be reserved for the world of adults. I know your studies suffered and that you lacked direction and guidance and recently got expelled from school. I believe the colloquial terminology is *flunked out*. In essence, you have been floundering the past seven years. You have become a lost soul in search of a guiding light. And I believe all these things transpired in your life not because of mere accident but because of a plan. Destiny, fate, ordained providence, call it what you may, is, after all, what brought you here to the PMRC. Do you believe such things, son? About destiny?"

"No, sir."

"Do you have religious beliefs of any kind? Do you believe the Almighty could have led you here?"

"No, sir. I don't believe He did. I believe you did with that telegram you sent me."

"Interesting. At least you understand my part in the plan. It's a start. So, do you understand what it is that I want you to do here?"

"All the telegram said was that you needed me to shoot predators killing off mustangs and that I would be rewarded handsomely."

"Yes. That's exactly what was stated. And, trust me, in the end you will be rewarded quite generously and derive a great deal of satisfaction from your deeds. Let me explain. For nearly twenty years, we have been attempting to eradicate the feral horse population from the Pryor Mountain range as part of *the-great-removal*. While the wild mustang may still carry a semblance of romantic old west Americana in the minds of some do-gooders, in actuality the horses are a plague. The beasts devour grasslands indiscriminately. They contribute to soil erosion and intensify the great dust bowl storms encountered lo these past ten years. They challenge our thriving cattle operations for prime land. In short, their time to leave has come. Our country is changing and no longer needs them. Fortunately, we are getting close, very close, to that lofty goal of ridding them off all Federal lands. Once we are finished here at Pryor Mountain, we will move onto Oregon and Nevada. We will not stop until the last mustang has been purged in body and in soul."

"Well, sir, how many we talking about?"

"Good question. In nineteen-nineteen there were over thirty thousand mustangs roaming a six hundred square-mile range stretching from this very spot east to the Bighorn River basin and north to Stratford Mountain and the Crow reservation. We believe we have reduced their numbers to fewer than one thousand that are spread among six herd populations and that all six are migrating into the Pryor Mountain meadowland region this summer. The problem we now face is that the remaining herds have wised-up, if you will, to our methodology. They possess a sixth sense and know we are out to dispatch them. This has posed a hardship for the drovers and my Judas stallion because the herds' bosses are putting up more resistance. The last of the bunch is becoming more elusive and more combative. And after so many devoted years, my Judas has become physically incapable of doing battle like he once did in his prime. So, what needs to be done to wrap up our venture this summer is to assist Judas. We need to rid the herds of their bosses at the outset of each roundup so Judas' only directive is to lure. Rid the herd of their leadership and the herd becomes easier to deceive and manipulate. This is where you come in, Mister Bartell. I need you to shoot the boss stallions. I need you to aid Judas so he no longer has to combat for supremacy. My crew of cowboys lacks your expertise, that of marksmanship at a distance of over a thousand feet. So, can I count on you to do my bidding? Will you allow me to become your employer and master?"

"Well, frankly sir, this ain't what I had in mind. Killing horses, that is."

"I am sure it is not."

"I thought I'd be killing the critters going after the horses."

"Your chance will come. Predators always follow the roundups. It will happen."

"But shooting horses just don't feel right."

"I understand. Putting down a creature as majestic as a wild mustang would pose a challenge to anyone of like mind. It could afflict one's conscience. But all things at the PMRC have a way of numbing that quandary."

"I just don't know."

"The choice is entirely yours, son. You are an adult now and this is an adult choice."

"I just don't—"

"Or you can always return back home and work with your brother."

"It's just—"

"Or, perhaps, you'd prefer to ride that boxcar and chase that ever elusive dream of freedom and California."

"But—"

"And did I mention the money?"

"No, sir. The telegram just said I'd be paid—"

"*Handsomely.*"

"Yes, sir."

"Then let me go into some detail in that regard. The Montana Cattleman's Association pays us three dollars a head for every mustang we dispatch. The United States Grazing Office pays us ten dollars. The J.B. Quick Company of Decatur Illinois guarantees us five cents per pound on the hook. And various horse byproducts operations we do business with from around this great nation pay a combined equivalent of three more dollars. That comes out to roughly forty-one dollars per horse, not counting the five dollars paid to us for dressing out the carcasses and prepping them for the reefer cars. I split the gross proceeds fifty-fifty with my crew. By the end of this summer, during the next three months of your labors, you could make over four thousand dollars. By September, you could be riding the rails first class instead of stowing away as a hobo. I believe four thousand dollars is more money than your family's funeral home garnered the past two years. It is nearly twice the annual income of the average American, the ones lucky enough to have gainful employment in these trying times. As you are aware, jobs for young men are almost impossible to find. In short, working for me beats poverty to hell and back. So, what say you, son? Can I count on you to do my bidding?"

The boy exhaled a long overdue breath and looked away from the shadow of Captain Belial. He gazed down the hallway and toward the newspapers on the walls, and wanted to run to the front door. What had he gotten himself into? He wondered. And just like the manic sentiments he felt when he made the decision to flee Billings, once again his world seemed lonely and bleak and full of despair. He knew riding the rails to California had been an aversion. He knew the true choice boiled down to working a job with dead people back at Billings or working a job at Potrero Gap killing already dead horses. Either way, with or without his help, the Pryor mustangs would die. He knew no one wanted wild horses alive anymore.

"I'll do it but just this summer. Not next year in Oregon or in Nevada or wherever else you're heading."

"Excellent choice, Mister Bartell. I knew you would make the correct one. Now, let us seal the agreement with the age-old custom of a handshake."

Captain Belial held out his trembling hand and the boy shook it. Then, with nothing else to say, the boy excused himself and headed back down the dark hallway for the door and the bunkhouse at the bottom of the hill.

"Oh. One more thing, Mister Bartell. Did I mention that you and our half-breed Chief will be assisted in your endeavors come this Monday?"

The boy turned around with a puzzled expression. "No, sir."

"Well, I have enlisted some of our latest twentieth century marvels to support you both. Rounding up mustangs will never quite be the same again."

"How do you mean, sir?"

"Ah-h-h. Wait until Monday. On Monday you shall see."

16

The lights of Laurel, Montana, shined brighter than anything Paris, France, could ever cast, at least in the minds of the PMRC cowboys. Post-prohibition and pre-Church of Christ, the south side of town drifted closer to drunken debauchery than Jesus. The favorite spot, Miss Edna's, served as both saloon watering hole and whorehouse. Every male in the area knew Miss Edna catered to an eclectic cliental ranging from county officials to clergy to cowboys, all under the same roof and usually at the same time on Saturday nights. Providing freebies to the sheriff's deputies never hurt business; providing indulgences for lovelorn clerics never hurt the souls of Miss Edna's wicked whores. It was at Miss Edna's where Bob kept good his promise to buy a round of women for his partners including the newest cowboy, Billy Bartell.

"So let me get this right, kid, you've never been with a woman? Never even seen a woman naked?" Bob pressed.

"No, sir, that's not what I said."

"It's okay, kid," Sully interrupted. "We all lose it sooner or later. Heck, I was with old Toothless that night he lost his. Fact is the girl's mother caught 'em right smack dab in the middle of the act."

"You're kidding."

"Nope. And I was embarrassed as all get out. I was," Bob chimed in.

"That's horrible. What'd her ma say?"

"Moo-o-o-o-o."

Bob and Sully doubled over in laughter. Bob slapped Sully on the back and pointed to Hayyel who refused to acknowledge the joke. Instead, Hayyel shook his head out of disgust at the opposite end of the bar, at a safe distance, downing shots of whiskey. About this same time, a tall mustached man heard the commotion and approached the three standing together. He took off his hat and squeezed the back of Sully's neck.

"You boys care to introduce me to your newest partner?"

Sully turned around cracking a smile. He recognized the man's tireless voice long before the turnaround. "Sheriff John Toms. How the heck are you?"

The sheriff laid his hat on the bar. He ordered another round of drinks for the PMRC cowboys, including Hayyel, and he shook the boy's hand. After the introduction, he recognized the boy's name, both because of the lad's notoriety as a local marksman and because of a history with the boy's parents. He began reminiscing, telling the boy about 'the good old days' when Isaac and Jennie and he and Martha, his wife of twenty-five years, attended public school together in Billings. He told how he, Martha and the boy's parents used to cut class to steal away to the sandbars on the Yellowstone River and go skinny-dipping. About how on one wintery day they stole his uncle Frank's Model-T and drove it all the way to Fry and back in a blizzard without getting stuck in the snow or caught by Uncle Frank. The year was 1913.

"In those days," he said, 'we were all young and foolish and madly in love. We didn't have two pennies to rub together but, poor as we were, we still had good times. We had each other and that's what mattered. Tell you one darned thing. Being best friends made living in this big empty Montana of ours worth all the tea in China. Those sweet memories make me a very rich man today. And I suppose, like most things in life, it had to come to an end. Once we all graduated, your ma and pa got married. I believe your older brother, Henry, had something to say about that. Your pa got all wrapped up starting his funeral business. He got a loan, bought the home and worked his hinny off. Your ma got tied down with the baby. About a year later, Martha and I got hitched. The two of us drifted down here to Laurel where I signed on as county deputy. So, by nineteen-fourteen our families had gone their separate ways. Never saw them again. They never saw us. Caught wind of your ma's passing and wrote your pa. Sent our condolences but we never heard back. Then, he got taken with consumption and we never got to say good-bye, at least the way we wanted to. Awful

sad about that, son. Awful sad. A few years back I got elected
Sheriff. And here I am." He paused and leaned back against the bar
railing. His lips buckled while his eyes stared at the floor recalling
the memories. "Boy, oh boy, I sure miss those days. I really miss
your ma and pa. They were good people. Darn good people. I'm
sorry they left this sweet earth of ours so young. Hope some day I
can see 'em again."

Sully spoke up deaf to the moment. "So, you gonna buy another
round, Sheriff?"

"Nope. I'm heading home to Martha. Just dropped by to check
on my deputies. Had to make sure they were getting taking care
of." He snatched his hat before turning to the boy. "Next time
you're in town, Billy, why don't you come by the house? We'll
have supper together. I'm sure Martha would love to meet you.
She speaks of your ma and pa all the time. We never had children
of our own. Having a young person in her midst will do her some
good, especially if it's the son of her best friend." He studied the
boy's face. "Anyone ever tell you you're a dead ringer for your
pa?"

"No, sir. A few have said I got his eyes."

"That you do, son. And a lot more of him, I reckon." The
Sheriff took out a wad of paper and scribbled his address on it and
handed it to the boy. "Anyone in town can give you directions to
where I live. Everybody knows me. Don't be a stranger. Hear?"

"Yes, sir."

"And try to stay out of trouble with these two scallywags." He
eyed Sully and Bob.

"Yes, sir."

As the Sheriff left the room, the boy noticed he shuffled with a
shoveled limp. Before he could ask anyone the question, Hayyel
sauntered from behind and spoke in his ear. "He took a fall off his
horse up in the mountains," he whispered. "The horse, it took a
tumble. Pinned him underneath. He was like that all night. Pinned
underneath. A pack of wolves tried to get to him and the horse.
The wolves, they killed his horse after he ran out of bullets."

"What happened to him? How'd he make it our alive?"

Hayyel smiled knowingly. "The white horse saved him."

By midnight the four cowboys had consumed enough alcohol that even Miss Edna, a sixty-year-old spinster-turned-madam, started appealing to their carnal instincts—especially Sully's. The boy had become so inebriated that a sixth beer swept aside any lack of self-confidence in the lovemaking arena.

"You know who'd be perfect for the kid?" Sully threw out in an exaggerated manner.

"Who?" Bob asked back, already knowing the answer to the setup.

"*Polly.*"

Bob's eyes lit recalling past romps. He twirled his handlebar moustache. "That one's a real B-girl sweetie. Sweet like a Georgia peach, she is."

Hayyel frowned ready to vomit. "How would you know? You have never been to Georgia."

"I know cuz I've eaten canned peaches and—"

"And what?"

"And I have a bibid imagination."

Hayyel grabbed his head as if in pain. "That is *vivid* imagination. Are you drunk or dumb?"

Sully stepped in-between the two, knowing Bob might ignite at those fighting words, but Bob kept his composure.

"Actually, I'm both," he stated after an exaggerated belch. "And I am also a sorry excuse for a cowboy." With that, Bob began to whimper. Sully put his arm around his friend to console him, too soused to verbalize his own sentiments.

With a sense of newfound courage, the boy stood up and moved to the stairwell leading to the bedrooms on the second floor. "What's her room number?" he asked, mumbling over a shoulder.

"Eight," all three shouted.

"And she's bought and paid for," Bob hollered out. "I knew she'd be the right one for you."

"Get to it, kid," Sully added.

"Have a good time," Hayyel blurted. "But remember, we must leave in four hours. Do not take all night."

17

The boy staggered up the stairs and fumbled his way down the hallway until he found the room. He knocked on the door twice before the voice inside beckoned, "*Entrée*." Inside he found the girl lying on the bed and waiting for him. She sprawled in a femme fatale pose, luxuriating in a full-length but sheer nightgown and acting every bit the part of a blond bosomy Mae West. He blinked a few times for a better gawk but her body shimmered in a sublime combination of light and shadow and she was hard to discern. The light radiated from an adjoining private bathroom; its door cracked ajar. The light bulb inside hung from a cloth-covered wire and swayed in the breeze from an open window, casting a shimmer on a tarnished but exquisitely beautiful creature. Likewise, the room played of contrasts and inconsistencies. At first, the boy smelled a sickening mix of cigarettes and lilacs, but the further he was drawn in, the place began to reek sweet and toxic moist and wonderful. It was then he noticed the phonograph had been playing all along. He recognized the melody from a Benny Goodman tune, *Moonglow*.

"Take off your boots and come join me, Toots," she said patting the bed.

Her voice sounded youthful but also experienced and contrived. Even the boy, given all his naivety, recognized the playacting one would expect of a well-heeled whore. But while the girl's voice lacked sincerity, it also hinted of little-girl coquettishness. He knew in an instant that there would be nothing special in the encounter other than a romp between sheets. She would tell him how virile he was and he would perform with all the gusto expected of a seventeen-year-old.

He sat on the chair and yanked off his boots, and tiptoed wobble-like to the bed with his head spinning. As he drew nearer and as his eyes fought to adjust to the light, he could finally make out her face, her blond bobbed hair and the robe that plunged in a 'V' to her navel. She lay on her side with one of her breasts exposed. He couldn't help but focus on the subtlety of its shape and on the worn dark rouge of her enlarged areola. Despite the alcohol-induced sweat cascading off his forehead, he felt himself slipping into full-blown sexual arousal.

"You're Miss Polly. R-right?" he asked, stammering.

"Yes," she answered. "And you must be Bob's lucky friend, Billy."

"Yes, Ma'am."

"So, how would you like to pleasure me, Billy? You on top or me?"

"Yes, Ma'am. Either way."

He stood at the edge of the bed still wearing his Montana hat, licking his parched lips and playing all the parts of every buffoon in search of that first awkward encounter. Like many an impatient virgin, he couldn't wait for her to respond and dropped his pants to his ankles and hopped on the bed, collapsing by her side.

"You've never seen a naked woman before, have you?"

He propped his head on his hand and attempted to appear suave but failed miserably. "I've seen plenty a naked women before."

"Really, Billy? You strike me as being new at all of this."

"I'm new at this alright."

"Then which it is, Toots?"

"I've seen naked women before. None as *lively* as you."

Struck by the boy's innocence, the girl decided to cease the playacting. What was the point? He reeked drunk and inexperienced but sweet. For those very reasons, she smiled at him with all the demur genuineness she could pull off and then reached out and took his hand. She thought about placing it tight against her breast the way she did with most gauche young men but, instead, decided to fold it with her own, finger interlaced with finger. Even with the insipid glow of the on-again-off-again light, the stale perfume that permeated the bedroom and the old Benny Goodman song, she sensed he was special and decided to take her time to help make his first sexual experience memorable.

"What would you like me to do?" she asked.

Without a hint of hesitation, the boy knew what was needed to get him in the right frame of mind. Like an old pro, he gave her specific instructions. He told her to wash off her makeup, lie flat and naked on her back and not move a muscle. "Be still and close your eyes. And put your hands to your sides lifeless-like," he added.

She thought the request strange but since she had honored many odd requests in her profession, she obliged him by withdrawing to the bathroom and scrubbing the makeup off. Upon her return, she lay on her back with her eyelids shut and her arms drawn up limp to her hips. She tried not to move or flinch or breathe yet, at the same time, tried to hold back a snicker or two. The albino-like whiteness of her skin seemed to illuminate the room even more and helped the boy with his task.

Once he felt satisfied with her positioning on the bed, he sat up on his knees and stared down at her body. "You are b-b-beautiful," he kept stuttering. "So beautiful."

He ran his hands down her body from her throat to her feet. He examined her in the same manner as he had other women before, but in a far different setting. He noticed how her breasts drooped and had once given nourishment to an infant and the random-pattern stretch marks that wormed across her slight paunch. He touched the lacerated bite marks on her inner thigh and the yellowish-blue strangle bruises to her slender neck and the purple hickies splashed across her shoulders. He rubbed his fingertips across the red and brown needle track bumps in the creases of her arms and felt the gnarled misshapen ulna bone once snapped by a former customer. And as he looked at her lying there peacefully, he wanted to cry. The girl had journeyed to hell and back but somehow survived to make it to this night with him.

"How old are you?" he asked.

She kept her eyes closed and answered him as if in a trance. "How old do you think I am?"

"Fifteen. Sixteen tops."

The girl's eyes popped open. "How old are you?"

"Seventeen."

"Seventeen? Jeepers. You're seventeen and the only man who's ever guessed my age. How'd you know?" She asked the question purely bewildered, for no one before had ever come within five years of guessing correctly. She had kept her true age a secret for fear of losing the job. Besides, none of her customers really wanted to know the truth about her status as a minor.

"I've seen plenty a girls like you before. Too many times." He paused and felt her stomach and the stretch marks again. "How old's the baby?"

This time she startled. She sat up straight, wrapping the bedspread around her body, and then fell back hard against the headboard with her knees tucked against her chest. "How do you know these things?" she asked.

"Ain't hard," he stated. "All you got a do is read the signs. A little somethin' I picked up at my old job. Been doing it since I was ten." Judging from the look on the girl's face, he knew his words had done little to console her fright. "It's okay. I grew up a little too fast, too," he restated, trying to console her with a half-smile but the smile didn't work, and he moved in closer and held her in his arms. He kissed her forehead and told her he didn't think it would be proper for them to make love. He told her about growing up in Billings and about his brother raising him at the funeral home and about how darned much he missed his ma and pa. When he finished telling her his brief life history, he asked her how much time Bob had paid for. She told him until dawn. "So, what do you wantta do until then?" he asked.

"I know," she said. Her face lit up. "Let's get out of here, Billy. Let's go to the movies."

"But the theater is gonna be closed. It's way after midnight."

"Nonsense. It never closes."

She jumped out of bed and shimmied on a tight fitting silk crepe garden dress without a thought to putting on underwear, and strapped up two bright red wide-heel pumps. "Put those boots back on," she ordered. "We're going on a date. A real date."

They bolted out the second floor fire escape and fast-walked three blocks to downtown Laurel where the Rialto still lit up majestically in a fiery burst of incandescent strobe and neon. The theater's spire towered ten feet higher than the rest of the two-story art deco facade and resembled a red-green-yellow neon-laced rocket ship. The movie house served both as entertainment and as area landmark. Folks in Billings twenty miles east claimed the theater rivaled the Aurora Borealis on a warm summer night.

The two of them stood mesmerized in front of the theater, gawking at the lights, holding hands, but the theater spread empty of humanity.

"Like I said. It's closed."

She ignored the boy's remark and yanked hard on his hand, leading him into the alley where a back stairway led to the second floor roof. "Come on, Billy," she said. "You've got to see this."

The flat roofline sloped upward to the building's front facade and to the rocket ship aglow in unappreciated pageantry. She ran ahead, leaned over a railing and raised her arms in deference to the lights. "I love this," she shouted, turning to the boy whose face washed in neon rainbow. "Someday, Billy, I'm going to make it to Hollywood and become a big star and live the glam life. Then, you'll see my name on the marquee. You'll see this gorgeous mug next to Gable's and Tracy's and you'll say, *ain't she grand.*"

Before the boy could say anything, she spun back around, discarding her dress in a tumbled heap on the roof. She began dancing pagan-naked in homage to the movie gods looking down from heaven. The boy took off his hat and placed it across his heart. He watched her gyrate under the moon and the lights, dancing to the Benny Goodman tune still playing inside her troubled head. She was like no one he had ever met before. "I thought you was purdy grand the first moment I laid eyes on you, Polly," he said. But she didn't hear his words, being too preoccupied with her dream and her twirling and dancing and the heroin high feeding her flight of fancy.

18

By sunrise, the white horse, known both as Old White and as Remliel, hid motionless behind a giant cedar near the crest of Pryor Mountain. He had been laying-in-wait for the right opportunity to overthrow the boss of an unknown herd and become the new leader. It was the first herd he had stumbled upon once he left Black Mesa. Given the situation, he had little time to be selective as to which herd to steal. Man had already gained dominion over all the wild mustangs on the mountain. Any remaining herd would do just fine. Off in the distance his rival sipped from a creek for the third time without consuming any water. Each time the herd's boss posed ready to swallow, it became spooked and jerk-raised its head with water cascading from its parched muzzle. The rival knew a challenger lurked somewhere in the distance. The scent in the air said as much. After the fourth attempt to sip, the boss grew impatient and pawed the creek in a showy 'I know you're out there' defiance. Still, the white horse stood his ground and refused to challenge prematurely.

Through it all, the white horse's hind leg throbbed unmercifully. He knew what little speed could be mustered for a charge would be short-lived. Instead, he would wait for the boss to seek him out and then attack from behind the bush. Too much exertion too quickly might expend what little energy remained after the tedious two-day climb up the mountain. If he reared to stomp, his hind legs might collapse under his weight. Bucking would worsen the condition. That left biting and frontal assault his only tactical weapons.

He had gone without food during the hasty ascent. His exposed ribs reflected how gaunt and weak he had become with the ordeal. Rivals knew a challenger's vulnerabilities from body language and signs like visible ribs. It would be best to hold off revealing his sad state until the last second. In any case, he knew the herd's survival depended on his resolve, for they knew nothing of man's ways. They knew nothing of what lay below the gap in the mountain or of man's voracious appetite to kill their kind. And if he won this impending battle, he would lead the herd as far from the kill chutes as possible.

By noon, the boss had grown impatient and miscalculated the unseen challenger. As it rounded the corner upwind from the giant cedar, it failed to locate the white horse's scent, and bobbed for the smell lost seconds earlier. That was the exact moment the white horse rammed, tumbling it backward and snapping its hind leg tendon.

Less than an hour later, the white horse had gathered the herd and begun the task of pushing them north and east. Before cresting the summit, he looked back over a shoulder. His rival lay on its side unable to stand. Days later, the once invincible stallion would still be there for the buzzards. They would feast on its flesh and devour the mighty hulk that once commanded the respect of over one hundred and fifty fellow mustangs. The old king that once ruled so confidently was as good as dead. Watching the horse struggle, the white horse felt an uneasy kinship. He watched the horse squeal trying to stand and then collapse again in agony. There was nothing he, the winner, could do to change the inevitable fate of the loser. Instead, he would focus all his energy on the mission, that of marching the herd to where the lights of the city glowed seven years earlier. The country north was safe. It lay abundant with grass, water and open range. It was the land of miracles, where a mountain lion exploded in the air and a two-legged boy-creature waved and shouted *God Bless You*. Yes. To the north is where he would lead them.

XIX

I was four years old when I saw my first live horse. It was at my grandpa's farm. Now you would think living in Billings Montana in nineteen twenty-six there woulda been horses everywhere but truth of the matter is even back then they'd all been replaced. Places like Billings. Most farms and ranches. Most everywhere. Common folk just didn't need horses anymore. Everything had gotten mechanized. Hard to believe it happened so fast. But it did. That's why the first time I ever laid eyes on a real horse was at my grandpa's farm. So what I'm about to tell you is a combination of things. Some from memory. Some from stories passed down to me when I got older. And some a little from my imagination. But here it goes:

When my Ma took ill my Pa sent me away for a few weeks to live with his parents on their farm. They lived halfway between Billings and Bozeman about five miles south of Columbus. Half a day's train ride in those days. They were second generation wheat farmers. Anyways. I remember my grandpa showing me around the farm and him telling me about his one and only remaining horse being sick and dying. The horse's name was Papa as in Paw-Paw on account he could do trick counting by pawing the ground with his hooves when you held up fingers. Three fingers and he'd paw the ground three times. And so on. Real smart horse. But that day Papa was in his stall rolling over-and-over moaning and groaning in a whole lot of pain. "What's wrong with him," I asked to which my grandpa says, "He's got the colic. There's nothing I can do for him. I'd shoot him and put him outta his misery but I don't got the heart. He'll be dead by daybreak, anyways." Now being only four I

didn't understand bout dying or colic or such things. I just saw a
horse in a lotta pain and there was nothing I could do to help him
out. Just standing there watching old Papa dying tore my grandpa
up something fierce. To get away from the sight of it all he took my
hand and led me to a bluff by the river. From that spot we could
see his entire field of golden wheat and the farmhouse and silo and
that big old barn. The land stretched as far as the eye could see.

And he turns to me and says, "Billy, I took over this farm thirty
years ago from my pa. In those days we was dirt poor. We had a
plow and an ox and that was about it. Only tilled forty acres of
bottomland. We wasn't gettin much plowed under cuz the ox
always come up lame and it was backbreaking work for a
sodbuster like me to do it on his own. So, one day I got an idea and
headed south to the hills and rounded up some mustangs to help
work the fields. That was the way it was. If you needed a horse you
went out, run your traps, and caught you a free one. Caught many
a horse that way. But in nineteen ought-one I went down there for
the last time. Already had three good ones. Just needed one more.
Within a day I'd tracked down the biggest and strongest yearling
in the herd. I needed a strong horse to help pull the plow. Didn't
wantta foal or an old one set in its ways. Wanted a yearling.
Easiest to break. When I caught him he put up one hell of a fight. I
cinched his legs and left him on the ground for three days till he
got good and dry and hungry. I let him know from the get-go who
was boss. That bein' yours truly. Then I cut him loose and fed him
and took good care of him. Never did ride him though. Don't think
he could ever be ridden far as that goes. He was a working horse
plain and simple. Now, you know who that horse was?"

"Papa," I said.

"That's right. Papa. And for the next twenty years that horse
worked his tail off for me. He never complained. Never wallowed
in self-pity. Just did his job. Look about you, Billy. All this land. All
six hundred forty acres that horse plowed under with me yellin'
gettyup from his backside and him takin orders good as any
soldier. Couldn't of done it without him. A few years back I bought
the gasoline tractor and the mechanical combine and decided I
didn't need old Papa no more. He was the last of a great bunch.

The other horses havin' already died off. And I didn't know what to do with him, so I trailered him ten miles south and took him up to the hills where he come from and I turned him loose. Thought he'd be better off free than cooped up where he wernt needed. A few days after I got home your grandma says, Jonathan, look who come back. I looked out the kitchen window and it was Papa. That's when I realized that Papa's home was this farm and not the wilds. I realized that he and I were like kindred souls tied to this very spot. He couldn't leave it anymore than I could. So, I corralled the old boy up and that's where he's been these past six years. He's twenty-seven years old now and a rarity age-wise for horses like him. And now, after all this time, it looks like we're finally gonna lose him and I've never properly thanked him for all the good he's done this family. And I am ashamed of myself for it."

I remember my grandpa falling to his knees and crying out loud and holding me tight and his heart breaking and me telling him how everything was gonna be all right.

That night I couldn't sleep. Seeing my grandpa all upset like that. Seeing that poor old horse in so much pain. I couldn't stand it. So I stole down to the barn. And I remember seeing Papa shivering and cold and frothing at the mouth. Suffering horrible. That's when I grabbed a horse blanket and threw it over him and laid on top of him to keep him warm. I remember telling him that he couldn't die cuz grandpa had something important he wanted to say. And I rubbed his neck and stroked his ears and kept him warm all night long.

Next morning my grandpa came out to the barn sure he was gonna find Papa dead. Instead he found me riding him bareback in the corral wearing nothing but my PJs and a big old grin.

"Billy," he says, "what in blue blazes did you do?" To which I said, "I fixed him."

I'd never seen my grandpa so happy. He walked straight up to that horse and he threw his arms around its neck and he kissed it smack dab on the nose and says, "Thank you for many good years. You're my friend and I will never forget you. Ever."

Papa died two years later. Grandpa used his tractor to dig out a pit for the grave behind the house. We all came for the funeral.

Three years later grandpa died and we buried him next to his horse. As the saying goes: one good horse is all a man ever needs in a lifetime. Guess Grandpa found his.

20

When the Beechcraft Staggerwing buzzed the camp for the third time, the cowboys scrambled out of the bunkhouse to watch the acrobatic commotion. The single engine aircraft soared low in the midday sun. Its bi-wing, closed-cockpit design was the latest advancement in the emerging private aircraft industry. The bright yellow bird swooped upside-down over the entrance road and away from the mountain, then flipped one-eighty, almost slamming into the ground before leveling out to a bump landing and a dusty stop. Ten feet separated the craft's propeller from the massive Π-shaped entrance. The cowboys hustled down to where the plane parked. Lieutenant Mullin opened the cockpit door and climbed out. The pilot, a short scrappy man named T. Fenneus Johnson III (or, simply T.F.), shut off the engine and hopped out, chasing after Mullin. When he caught up, both men strutted to the gathered cowboys; both acted quite pleased with themselves. Sully fired off the first salvo.

"Where the heck did you get that aeroplane?"

"Rented it." Lieutenant Mullin answered without missing a stride. "We've got it the rest of the summer. Captain's idea." He stopped long enough to survey his ragtag team. "And you must be the kid out of Billings. The sharpshooter."

The boy stepped up and introduced himself. The two shook hands. At six-feet, the boy towered over everyone in the crew but Mullin who sported fifty pounds more, most of it solid muscle, and another inch in height. He introduced the other man, the pilot, as an afterthought. Before the introductions finished, the cowboys were mauling the aircraft like children and ignoring the pilot's warnings about not touching.

"So what's the Captain aim to do with this thing?" Bob asked, yanking on the propeller. T.F. politely told him yanking on the propeller without the magneto turned off was not a smart thing to do. The warning didn't faze Bob.

The Lieutenant ignored the crew's mischievousness and told Bob he would answer all the questions after the cowboys lined up shoulder-to-shoulder facing him. He had some things they needed to discuss. Once they lined up, he proceeded to saunter in front with an inspection-like swagger. "Men," he said, "the Captain plans on finishing up this summer at Pryor Mountain and moving further west to Oregon. The only way we can accomplish his goal is with advanced tactical assistance. This plane will give us that. It will allow us to spot herds from a bird's eye view, communicate their location and initiate the elements of surprise and capture. With a little luck we'll be able to take back the mountain by the end of August and plant our flag on top."

The cowboys looked at each other with dumb-ass stares. *Take back the mountain?*

"Any more questions?"

The boy scratched his head and initiated a query when, in fact, 'Any more questions' really meant 'Do not ask any more questions.'

"Yes, sir. I was wondering how you're gonna communicate to us where the horses are at? I mean, you being in the airplane and us being on horseback and such."

Hayyel spoke up. "Yes. Lieutenant. That does not make sense."

Sully piped in, "Unless you think we're telepathic. And telepathy didn't work too darned well for old Houdini."

"Houdini is dead, nimrod." Bob threw out.

"Of course he's dead. I knew that. I was just bein' humorous—"

"Both of you are out of line. Now fall back and shut up," the Lieutenant barked.

By now, T.F. had returned from the cargo hold, lugging a weighty backpack with a thin-wire mast antenna protruding from its top flap. He spoke up. "This, gentlemen, is how we're going to communicate. It's a newly designed Canadian Army Air Corps field backpack two-way radio. It's called a 'walkie-talkie' and it works like a private communications machine. Some of you will be to the rear carrying this pack and the others will be with me scouting from the air. I will communicate with the ground echelon from the airplane radio when we locate a herd. Abracadabra. Stone age horses meet modern *tele*-cowboy."

Hayyel still acted confused. "So, how is this going to work?"

The Lieutenant butted in. "You and the boy will ride with T.F. When you spot a herd, T.F. will land you in close proximity. He says he can land the plane anywhere the length of a football field and he just proved it by landing on the road. You'll track the herd on foot until the rest of us can catch up by horseback. You'll call in your coordinates utilizing your radio. When we get close, the kid shoots the boss and I release Judas to do his job. Plain and simple. Any more questions?"

Bob threw down his hat. "Tain't fair. It's cheatin'. Them horses won't know what hit 'em. I like the old ways better. I like the cowboyin' ways. I don't like all this here technical change."

Hayyel corrected him. "That's *technological* change."

"I don't care what it's called. I still don't like it."

"Hell. What's next, Flash Gordon?" Sully piped up, pointing his finger at the Lieutenant all googly-eyed crazed. "Death rays? Ropes made of light beams. Dick Tracy telephone wrist watches and moving pictures through the air?"

"Tell you one damn thing. When all that happens there'll be no need for us cowboys," Bob shouted. "When that happens this old country of ours will have one foot in the crapper and one in the grave."

Hayyel grinned sarcastic. "No need for cowboys? Sounds good to me."

The boy spoke up. "I don't know if I can carry that communication thing. It looks real heavy. Looks like it weighs more than me and I got a sore lower back. I weigh one forty-five, one fifty tops and my rifle ain't too light neither. . ."

Bob took out the lucky penny and flipped it in the air while Sully called it. Loser had to tote the radio backpack. Hayyel started a Crow war dance just to irritate the Lieutenant. The boy was still yakking nonstop.

T.F. looked at Mullin and then at the four cowboys, each one a circus act unto themselves. "You were right, Lieutenant. Nut cases. Everyone of 'em."

21

The Beechcraft climbed to eight thousand feet and leveled out bearing due east toward the mountain. The boy and Hayyel hunched in the back seats pressed against opposite windows, looking down as the ground faded into small clumps of green. Within a few minutes, the reverse happened as the hills and mountainside climbed to their elevation. Treetops skimmed the bottom wing and T.F. raised the craft's nose to avoid collision.

The other cowboys got a head start two days earlier. Hayyel was first to sight the three men with the packhorses, Judas, and their two horses saddled and readied. T.F. steered the craft past the ground team again so the boy could get a better look. From their birds eye view the boy said he could make out Sully and Bob flipping them off as they soared by.

Farther east and north, the tree line thinned and opened up to a broad expanse of meadow. Little snow remained and wildflowers danced in a sea of green tundra. Creeks brimmed with tumbling water. The boy claimed he could see trout spawning upstream. Higher up and less than two and a half miles from the ground team, they spotted the first mustangs. When T.F. buzzed the herd, the horses froze, unsure of the noisy yellow bird's intent. If horses could gawk, over one hundred fifty gawked in unison as if synchronized.

T.F. kept his course true north in pursuit of an accurate count of the herds at the higher elevations. Sure enough, a little farther on they located a second and third herd. On the east side of the mountain, the boy saw a fourth bunch nearing the crest and heading southwest. A fifth herd scrambled over rocks but they found no sixth group. T.F. hollered above the roar of the single engine, "Where's the sixth herd? The Lieutenant says there's supposed to be six. I counted five."

Hayyel shouted back, "I do not know. Can you make a bigger sweep of the mountain?"

T.F. took the plane higher to twelve thousand feet. At that altitude, they had a more commanding view of the ground. He started five miles out from the mountain's jagged peak and swung around counter-clockwise in a broad circle. When he completed the first pass, he moved farther out. The sky churned blue and the visibility perfect for spotting anything that moved below. On the second pass, they observed the ground team as small dots. On the third pass, Hayyel thought he saw some movement north. T.F. banked the plane for a closer look. From less than two miles away, Hayyel spotted the sixth herd and instructed T.F. to approach the horses at treetop level for a closer look.

"What's wrong?" the boy asked.

"They are moving away. The wrong way."

"Away from what?"

"Pryor Mountain"

"Why?"

Hayyel shrugged his shoulders.

"Where are they going?"

"I think they are moving as far from the mountain as possible. *They know*."

"They know what?"

"They know about us. They are fleeing."

"How about the other herds? How come they're not following?"

Hayyel pressed his nose against the window again as T.F. banked the plane. His eyes stared at the ground and then shifted back to the boy. "The other herds do not have wise leaders. This one is wise."

"Which one?" The boy climbed over Hayyel to look out the same window.

"That one," Hayyel said, pointing out the white horse. "His name is Remliel. He is taking them where it is safe."

"And where's that?"

"North, where they can't be hunted. To the Crow reservation."

22

They circled back to the location of the first herd. T.F. landed the Beechcraft in a meadow on the backside of a low hill, opposite the spot where the mustangs had been grazing. Hayyel and the boy loaded up their equipment and agreed to share in carrying the weighty radio backpack. Hayyel went first. They watched T.F. take off, bank the plane back toward camp and vanish over the horizon, leaving them on their own.

Once they hiked to the top of the hill, they saw the herd spread out below them in a three-hundred-yard swath. More than once Hayyel remarked how easy the hunt was progressing and how he liked not having to camp out for days at a time to scout horses with Sully yakking the entire time. The boy, he said, was much quieter. They dropped their gear by a tree and crawled to the last line of firs bordering the large meadow. Hayyel thought he spotted the herd's boss farther down. They began dashing in-and-out behind the trees' broad trunks, working their way along the meadow's incline to the rear. Along the way Hayyel broke out the binoculars and scanned the area, noting where the lead mare roamed, the broodmares nested and the yearlings lagged. The herd appeared content, taking its time devouring grass and in no hurry to leave the area. The open meadow would be the perfect spot to stage the ambush. He told the boy to go back and call in their location based on T.F.'s reckoning with the map. Meanwhile, he would remain behind and continue to scout for the boss stallion.

Both the boy and Hayyel received training on the two-way radio, but the boy seemed to have more of a knack for operating it. The radio took all of five minutes to warm up its vacuum tubes. After another minute of static and humming, a whistle-like whirling sound took over until the receiver-modulator detected a distant signal. Then it could broadcast human voices.

"Ground crew. Ground crew. Do you read me?"

"*I'll be. It's the kid on the walkie-talkie.*" Sully's voice boomed through the airwaves. "*Hell, yes, we read you, kid. Loud and damn clear. Roger that. Bob do you believe this? It's the kid. Roger, kid. Roger.*" Sully accidentally locked the microphone switch on the handset and the boy could hear everything.

Bob grabbed the handset out of Sully's hand. "*Who the heck is Roger? The kid's name is Billy.*"

In the background Billy heard Sully saying, "*You numb-nuts. I know what the kid's name is. You say 'Roger' when you understand what the other person has said. It's part of two-way radio etiquette. Don't you know nothin'? You raised in a barn?*"

Bob must have been nodding his head he understood because he didn't fire off a retort. "*So, how the hell are you, kid?*"

"I'm fine. Where's Lieutenant Mullin?'

"*He's takin' a shit. We're in charge. Least ways for now.*"

There was no time to wait for the Lieutenant's return, so the boy gave his report. "We landed about half an hour ago. Found a good-sized herd. Based on the map, you fellas should be about two miles southwest of us. Hayyel says to come up Shreffler's draw. That way the herd won't see you. When you get to where it forks, go due west two hundred yards and you'll be at the northern tip of the meadow where the herd's grazing. You'll be above the herd. We'll be below. Hold up there in the trees. We'll radio you when it's time to release Judas or if you hear a gunshot, release him. Whichever comes first. Be ready by high noon. Copy?"

Bob still hogged the handset. "*Roger. We copy. High noon it is. Roger. Roger. Roger. Say, kid, do I sound like Jack Benny?*"

The boy had already turned off the radio on the second *Roger* and thrown the backpack over his shoulders. He left the bedrolls by the tree but grabbed the rifle and took off to return to his partner.

Hayyel had moved farther down the incline and now lay spread-eagle on a flat-topped boulder about eight feet off the ground. He glassed the herd, counting and counting again. The boy asked him where the boss hunkered and Hayyel tossed him the binoculars pointing to the far side of the meadow and a rare saw-tooth maple.

The boy scanned the tree and, sure enough, in the shade hid the brave leader standing asleep. The boy guessed the distance to be eighteen hundred feet.

"How the heck am I supposed to shoot him all the way over there?"

"Be patient, boy. He will move our direction and follow his mares. They always follow the mares."

The boy looked higher up the meadow. The herd was slow motion grazing north toward the base of the mountain.

"But I told the others to be ready to release Judas by noon. What if he doesn't come out?"

"He will come."

"But how do you know?"

Hayyel was finding his new partner almost as annoying as Sully. "You are ignorant, boy. Be patient. Be quiet."

The boy said nothing more. He slouched behind the boulder and started prepping the rifle. Hayyel watched the lad fumble with the bolt-action mechanism. "Do not worry, boy. It will come to pass," he said. Nevertheless, the boy ignored Hayyel's words, being too preoccupied with the thought of killing his first horse.

Two hours later the boss stallion emerged from the shade of the maple. His harem had already sauntered an eighth of a mile up the inclined meadow and, after shaking himself awake, he decided to slow trot follow. He struck a serpentine course along the way, scouting for tender clover overlooked by the marauding hoard, and managed to find a few tasty leftovers. As he neared the boulder where Hayyel and the boy hid, his ears perked and he stood motionless looking their direction. Something had caught his attention.

The boy sunk low on his knees and slid off his hat. "You think he knows we're here?" Hayyel shook his head 'no' but still kept an eye on the horse, peeking from around a corner and underneath a jutting rock. For the next ten minutes, the horse kept up the bug-eyed trance and then, convinced something indeed lurked behind the boulder, crept to within fifty yards for a better view. Hayyel checked his pocket watch. In two minutes it would be noon. The horse stood too close. It would hear the warm-up hum on the walkie-talkie.

"You need to take the shot now," Hayyel whispered.

The boy flipped the aperture sight away from the iron sight and leveled the rifle. From fifty yards the aperture wasn't needed. Any fool could make an unaided shoulder kill from that distance. Any fool but the boy.

"Why do you not take the shot?" Hayyel pressed.

The boy said nothing. His sweaty palms and interminable lip licking said everything.

"Boy. Have you never killed anything other than that one mountain lion?"

"No. Just the lion."

Hayyel looked disgusted and yanked the rifle out of the boy's hands. He jerked up off his knees and took a clear shot, dropping the horse where it stood. He tossed the rifle back. The boy caught it one-handed and then stood, eyeing the kill with a most shamed expression. Hayyel poked him in the chest, infuriated. "Do not tell anyone about this. Understand? You shot the horse. Not me. We were up there." He pointed to the hill three hundred yards behind them where the trees clumped in a thicket. "You are ignorant, boy. When you stop being ignorant you might become a human being. You have a long way to go."

The boy stammered. "Yes, sir. I'm sorry. I just couldn't do it."

"This time it is okay. Next time, from a thousand feet away, I will not be able to pull the trigger for you. Grow some balls, boy, and grow them fast. You cut a pact with the Captain. Now keep it."

Everything else in the roundup went as planned. When the cowboys heard the gunfire, they released Judas who charged to the front and reversed the herd's course. The cowboys followed the black stallion's lead and pushed the mustangs back down the meadow and toward Potrero Gap. The boy and Hayyel met up with the crew, climbed aboard their horses and assisted in the drive the rest of the way down the mountain. Everyone was amazed at how effective the first airborne-assisted operation went. No one ever suspected the boy had yet to make good on the deal he struck with

Captain Belial. Three nights later, they corralled the mustangs in the stockyards and the Captain kept good his tradition of honoring the horses with an executioner's rhapsody.

23

Twenty years of capturing wild mustangs had turned horse slaughtering at the PMRC into an exacting science. The cowboys acquired their first bit of wisdom through random test and analysis, back in 1919. The result: never line up more than eight horses in the kill chute. Shortly thereafter, a logical corollary followed: selectively choose which horses to line up. The key was to identify family units or, in horse vernacular, 'bands.' As long as a band stayed together on their way to the gallows, walking-dead horses more willingly capitulated to the gun.

Skittish, spooked, panicky—words used to describe a horse about to be put down, too often became synonymous with other words—loco, combative, dangerous. Frequently, cowboys got kicked, bitten, stomped or butted by a horse desperate to escape. Hence, the axiom the cowboys worked by, *the calmer the horse, the safer the slaughterman*, motivated their scientific queries.

After six more years passed, the crew stumbled upon the benefits of blindfolds and head tie downs. Tying horses' heads nose-down tight against their chests in combination with blindfolding offered less opportunity for the horse to become violent. Horses unable to lift their heads cannot rear up or bite. The tactic also better positioned the horse's forehead for the gun.

By year ten, the crew determined that keeping horses touching nose-to-flank provided a needed (false) sense of security in the chute. The more secure a horse felt, the easier to separate, shackle and render unconscious.

After the fifteenth year, the crew discovered that classical music squelched any remaining residual fears horses experienced in their holds. Played at an ear-shattering volume, music masked the screams and whinnies of horses about to be killed. Captain Belial typically played string concertos and discovered Mozart's worked best.

Lastly, early-on in year twenty (1939), Lieutenant Mullin read in *The Bovine Quarterly* how utilizing a 'bell gun' versus a regular handgun improved the odds of keeping an animal alive but unconscious during the dressing out process. It made sense that the gun could also work on horses. Keeping the heart pumping through exsanguination was not only desirable but also healthy; pumping out residual blood rid a carcass of latent bacterial diseases and helped ward off potential spoilage.

The bell gun began replacing bolt guns and revolvers in the late 1920s in most American cattle slaughterhouses. The handheld single-shot .22 caliber pistol had an expanded bell-shaped muzzle that, when pressed against an animal's thick skull, protected the slaughterman from ricochet. With a .22 short cartridge, the bullet uniformly penetrated the cranium by no more than two inches and rendered an animal unconscious. The gun had never been designed to kill. Once shot, the horse would collapse, shackled and suspended by a hind leg, while its heart continued to beat after throat slitting and until its death.

24

With one mustang remaining in the kill chute, Sully reached in between the fence railings and wrapped the drag-away chain around the horse's hind leg. He pulled slack from the overhead hoist and the chain went taut drawing the horse's leg backward and up in the air toward the hoist and the abattoir slide-rail. Frozen in that position and with its head drawn tight against its chest, the horse stood on three legs wincing in pain. After days without food and water, it languished, too exhausted to resist. Sully climbed over the chute to the front platform where Bob stood holding a pocket watch. With sighs of relief, both men nodded to each other and then glanced at the time on the watch. Hayyel, the boy, and Lieutenant Mullin were busy at their assembly line stations and oblivious to the work being near its end. The pair observed Hayyel run the ten-inch blade of his Indian hunting knife along the neck of an unconscious upside-down horse. Blood shot out in rhythmic spurts into a steel barrel already brimming with blood. They watched the Indian chant the same mysterious Crow words he had used thousands of times before, and cut off the horse's mane and throw it into one of two canvas satchels sitting by the barrel. As Hayyel's horse continued to bleed out, he took a hacksaw to the horse's front hooves and tossed the first one into a wooden crate.

Bob pointed out Lieutenant Mullin whose shirt drenched in blood and who had just finished gutting his horse. They watched the boy cart away entrails in a wheelbarrow to the pit they had dug the day before. Beyond that fresh pit, row after row of dirt mounds dotted the landscape like a massive graveyard, a grisly reminder of previous slaughters.

"I suppose we oughtta go help those boys after we're finished with this here one," Sully stated deadpan. He spat some chaw on the last horse to be killed, without thinking twice where the spatter might flop.

"I suppose that'd be the right thing to do, Compadre. Mighty white of you to think good on them. You're all heart."

"Well, I just know that Lieutenant Mullin is gonna need some help with the hides."

"Indeed."

"And they do look awful tired-like. Especially the kid."

"No more than you and me. Shoot. We've been at it just as hard and just as long."

"True."

"So, why don't we just let them work unaided a bit longer for the experience and thrill of it?" Bob asked, casting the question with a sarcastic smirk.

Sully gazed back at Hayyel's upside-down horse still pumping out blood. "How just long did you wager it'd take?"

"I said that big a horse, even peaked as it looks, would pump out in under two minutes. You said it'd take over two. And I believe we put up our favorite Indian head penny on the wager."

"And what's it been?"

Bob checked his pocket watch again. His face wrinkled. "I believe you're gonna get the penny back."

Sully moved to the last horse in the kill chute. He stroked it on the forehead. "Is this the spot where you put the bell gun?"

"You know it is. You've been watchin' me do it now for over a month. What you gettin' at?"

"Tell you what. I'll forego the penny if you'll let me pop him."

"What for?"

"Cuz I've never used the new gun and I wantta do it."

Bob thought it over for two seconds before cracking a wide toothless smile. "All righty. It's a deal. I keep the penny. You get to pop him." He handed Sully the gun and watched his friend lay the muzzle flat between the horse's eyes. "I guess after watchin' me do it, some of my professionalism bound to have rubbed off on you." He shifted Sully's hand and stood back. "Just remember, Compadre, it's all in the wrist."

As he said the words, Sully squeezed the trigger and the horse collapsed with the explosion. It swung away limp, suspended in the air by its shackled hind leg.

"Nothin' to this, Bob. Hell, you've been having all the fun while I've been bustin' my keister with the shackles. Not too fair, I'd say."

Bob refused to respond to what he figured was just another one of Sully's jealous tirades. He climbed over the chute, down the railing and opened up the side gate, sliding the suspended horse along the rail to the station where Hayyel worked. "Last one, Chief."

Still lazing on the platform, Sully feigned work empathy. "Say, there, Chief. You look awfully beat. Can I lend you a hand?"

"No. An hour ago, yes. Now, no."

"Ain't you still got a take them manes up the hill and do your mumbo-jumbo tonight?" Sully pursued.

"Yes. It must be done before sunrise."

"Well, maybe you should take the kid. Have him tote them heavy bags. Bob and me, we're too tainted and despicable to sanitize them horses with you. The kid's still a virgin. Nothin' happened the other night. Bein' a virgin oughtta count for somethin'."

Hayyel looked up at the sky. The night had turned misty cold with no stars visible. The moon hid somewhere in three-quarters phase behind low-hanging clouds, and the passage up the narrow trail would be cumbersome if not downright treacherous by foot. It all added up to hauling the two weighty satchels and the smaller bag with the rug and leather straps in the pitch-black with an unwieldy lantern for light. The prospect of accomplishing it alone seemed grueling and he was already exhausted. "Good idea, Sully. You are not as dumb as you look."

"Thank you kindly, Chief. I'll take that as a compliment."

25

Hayyel led the way through the darkness up Bopwadesh Hill. The boy struggled to keep pace with the surefooted Crow and stumbled climbing the rock-strewn switchbacks and descending into the shrub-littered gullies. With Hayyel the only one familiar with the trail and the only one permitted to carry the lantern, the boy had no choice but to stay close to his guide's heels.

"Are we there, yet?" the boy asked for the seventh time.

"We will be there when I say we are there, boy."

Hastily conscripted into the job, the boy still had no clue what had transpired. Hayyel refused to tell him anything. Bob and Sully just belly laughed when he threw the satchel of fetid horse manes over his shoulder. "Be sure and take a bath when you get back," they said. And they were right. He would need one. Yet, he also knew he owed Hayyel for taking the shot that killed the boss stallion and for keeping secret what really happened—how he chickened out. That alone obligated him to help the Indian scout, even if it meant exhaustion and reeking of dead horses. Now trudging half-delirious behind Hayyel, he didn't know what he was doing or where Hayyel was leading him.

"So, are you a real chief?" the boy asked, once again breaking the icy silence.

"Do I look like a chief?" Hayyel replied, agitated by the question.

"Then why do they keep on calling you that?"

"Because they are ignorant and will always be ignorant."

"Oh."

"And because they are from Texas."

The boy snickered at that one. "So, what's your real name?"

"Hayyel Gabriel."

"That's a nice name. Your pa, he must of been a white man."

"Yes."

"And your ma?"

"Full-blooded Crow."

"That figures." Having gotten Hayyel to communicate, the boy had to ask the question bugging him most the previous two hours. "So, what are we doing with these horse manes, anyways?"

"You will see and then you will understand."

"Okay. But why me and not one of the others?"

"Because you are young and you are strong." Hayyel stopped and spun around. His satchel swung wide and almost knocked down the boy. He held the lantern to the boy's face and spoke with sincerity. "And because your heart is good and your soul is pure." He turned back to the trail and resumed his hurried pace without saying anything else. The boy chased after.

"That white horse we saw from the airplane. You've seen him before. Right?"

"Yes. He has been in these mountains many years. He is a good horse. A wise horse."

"Well, how does he know. . .? I mean, why is he taking his herd north and—"

"I can not tell you how or why. Only He-That-Hears-All knows these things. As for me, I am just a human being. A Crow-Yankee human being." He waited a few seconds while dodging a log in the trail. "You are now talking too much, boy. Be silent."

"There's just one more thing I gotta say, then I'll hush up."

"And what is that?"

"Thank you."

"You do not need to thank me, boy. Just do the right thing when the day comes. Doing the right thing will be all the thanks I will need."

"What right thing?"

"The thing that will make you a human being."

"What are you talking about? What right thing?"

"Be silent. You are an ignorant boy. Even if I told you, you would not understand. Be content to know as little as possible for now. For it is written. And it shall pass. There is a plan and you are a part of it."

Though he wanted to ask a million more questions, the boy took the cue and remained quiet for the time being. When they reached the sacred spot at the top of the hill, he laid down his satchel next to Hayyel's and watched as the shaman tied the lantern to a low-hanging tree branch and spread an old Indian rug on the ground underneath the light. He said nothing when his guide stripped naked, sat cross-legged on the rug, and closed his eyes to meditate. Yet, after minutes of silence, the boy had to say something.

"You're doing a ceremony for them horses. Right?"

"Yes."

"Don't you need a full moon or something like that?"

"Yes, boy. But as you can see, the moon, it is not cooperating. So, I improvise. The lantern is the moon tonight. Okay? May I continue?"

"No. I wantta know more."

"Know what?"

"I wantta know why you kill horses. Crows love horses. Even I know that."

Hayyel shook his head. He knew silence played a loud impossibility with the lad. "Alright, boy. See if your brain can absorb this. . . *These horses were already dead.*"

The boy nodded his head, seeming to comprehend the statement. "You mean there was nothing you coulda done that woulda saved them from being killed, anyways."

"Yes. That is correct. If I kill them or not, they would still be dead. Someone else would do it. The plan had already been struck. The plan cannot be changed. My more important part in it is to set them free. Had I not been here to do that, their spirits would be lost."

"Lost?"

"Yes. Their souls would wander forever. I guide them to what you would call heaven. That is what I do here tonight."

"You get them mustangs into heaven, huh?"

"Yes."

The boy struck a skeptical pose even discernable through the lantern's dim glow.

"I can tell you do not believe in such things."

"About getting into heaven? Used to."

"That will change. When you become old and wrinkled you will ask yourself: *Was I a good man*? And when you lay on your deathbed, you will beg your god or any god to save your worthless soul. All white men behave like that. You become weak in death. And you become frightened. You are no different."

"It ain't gonna happen."

"No? Then be silent. Watch and learn from one who says 'it will pass.'"

The boy sat cross-legged next to Hayyel. He watched the shaman take a hunting knife from its sheath and cut off a strand of shoulder-length hair. He watched the man raise the knife high to the lantern in the right hand and raise the strand high in the left. He listened as Hayyel prayed aloud to the Crow giver of life and death, speaking the words always spoken at the horse ceremony:

> "My name is Hayyel Gabriel and I am a human being. I am the proud shaman son of Runs-With-Deer, daughter of the Crow Nation. I am the proud shaman son of Winston Gabriel, Yankee son of the city of New York and Federal Agent to the Crow people. I bleed Crow. I bleed Yankee. I bow to no man. I bow only to He-That-Hears-All. . . Tonight I bring You spirit horses to take into heaven so that the great Crow warriors with You may ride again."

Then Hayyel interrupted his conversation with his god, turned, and looked at the boy. "Sometimes human beings like me gather horse spirits to help horses get into heaven but sometimes horses gather human spirits to help men get into heaven. Remember that boy. It will serve you well."

The boy listened but said nothing. He remained silent until daybreak. Finally, after he and Hayyel had hung the last of the horse manes, they trudged back down the hillside and through the gap in the mountain to the stockades standing between heaven and hell.

26

Martha Toms must have been related to Will Rogers—she never met a stranger she didn't like. In this case, the stranger was Billy's tagalong girlfriend, Polly. Even before the two showed up for supper, Martha's husband, John, failed to mention the boy was bringing anyone. He also forgot to mention other minor details like his five deputies intimately knowing the girl, that she was a local prostitute hooked on 'black tar' and how she was striking beautiful. Worse, he had trouble keeping his eyes off Polly at the dinner table. Maybe it was the absence of a brassiere under the tight-fitting summer cotton dress attracting his attention. Maybe it was Polly's non-stop conversation. After all, being the center of any conversation suited Polly just fine. One thing, however, struck apparent and needed no explanation: cleaned up Polly looked all of her sixteen years of age. That revelation bothered the Sheriff for it finally occurred to him the girl could be a minor. Martha, on the other hand, found the girl's well-scrubbed youthful looks refreshing.

"So, dear, tell me again why you're spending the summer here with your Aunt Edna?" Martha asked the question as she passed a stacked mashed potato bowl to the boy.

"Well, Missus Toms, it's like this. My spinster Aunt Edna is a bit under the weather and needed someone to help her out with the business. She needed a working girl. Someone not afraid to put their back into their work. That would be me. I love working and putting my back into everything." As she continued to speak, Polly barefooted the boy under the table. Billy almost choked on a fried chicken wing.

"That's so terribly nice of you, Dear. I'm just surprised I don't know your aunt. Laurel is such a small town. Less than four thousand people and we usually know who's who. Which church does she go to?"

The girl shrugged her shoulders. "Gee-wiz. She hasn't been to church since I've been in town."

"Well then, maybe she'd like to go with John and me—"

"Martha," John snapped. "I don't think we should butt into other people's church business. It's not polite."

"Nonsense, John. Saving souls is always polite. It is what Jesus would want us to do."

"I don't think Jesus has anything to do with this, Martha." He turned to the girl broadcasting a daggered smile. "Isn't that so, Polly?"

The girl understood all too well. She smiled demurely at the Sheriff while her toes groped Billy's thigh. "Yes. You're right, John. As far as I know, my aunt could be a devil-worshipper. That would explain the Ouija board I found hidden under her bed."

Martha looked at John, then back at the girl. Billy's face had turned bright red. Something odd was going on between the three of them. Being left outside the secretive circle did not sit well with her. "Or, dear, maybe she's using the Ouija board for navigation." Martha deadpanned.

"Oh? And how's that?" the girl responded.

"Maybe she's using it to locate men." Martha looked from face-to face expecting a round of laughter. Instead, silence and startled stares. She turned back to the girl. "Well, dear, you did say she was a spinster, didn't you?"

John exhaled and Polly burst out laughing. Billy excused himself to vomit in the bathroom.

27

After supper the four retired to the screened back porch to escape the late afternoon heat baking the house. Martha served her famous apple pie á la mode. John had hand-churned ice cream earlier in the day and announced more than once how he now had to take three aspirins because his shoulder hurt so much. Next time Martha wanted ice cream, he said, Billy could do the churning. The boy interpreted the off-cuff remark as being positive—the Toms liked him and wanted to see him again. He felt good about them, too. It was Martha, however, who pampered Billy all afternoon and gushed over him. Seldom did she walk by the boy without brushing a shoulder or gazing at his eyes or languishing in the few words he uttered. "You remind me of you father," she finally blurted. "Seeing you brings back memories. I wish he was still alive. I miss him and your mother."

"Back in the day, your mother and I were best friends. Inseparable we were," she said. "One day during our junior year Jennie got an itch to meet your father. There were less than seventy in our class but for whatever reason Isaac had never spoken a word to her. He was shy and unsure of himself. Well, your mother kept making eyes at him and I could tell he wanted to talk to her. She was the prettiest girl in the school and he the most handsome. So, I decided to break the logjam. I walked right up to him and I said, 'Isaac Bartell, you are killing my friend. Shame on you.' Of course, he had no idea what I was talking about and wanted to know why Jennie was teetering on the throes of death. And I said, 'Jennie said she's going to hold her breath until you talk to her. Look at her over there. She's blue and about to expire.' Naturally, he wasn't about to let your mother pass out, and he must have known that I was just prodding him to get off his rump. So, he walked right up to her and he took her hand and he said, 'Jennie,

I've been waiting for this moment my entire life.' And he spoke with her and held her hand and stole her heart right then and there. Now, you might think those words of his were corny or pre-planned but you had to know your father. He meant every spontaneous word of what he said. It came straight from his heart. He had been waiting his entire life to talk with the love of his life. He knew she was the one."

Martha started to get misty eyed and John took her hand and squeezed it. "Like I told you before, son," he said, "your ma and pa were good people."

Later, as the Sheriff limped back onto the porch juggling a second bowl of ice cream for the guests, Billy pressed the question on his mind most of the afternoon. "Sir, do you mind telling me about how you came to get that bad leg of yours?" It was a veiled question. The boy really wanted to know about the white horse. "Sure," the Sheriff answered. "I'd be more than happy to tell you about it."

"It was five years ago almost to the day when the accident happened," he said. "I went hunting for elk up in the hills south of town. I took my horse, Dusty, and my bedroll, my revolver, some provisions and my hunting rifle. Didn't take a whole lot of ammunition though. Wish I had, now. But I didn't and that's just the way these things turn out. So, Dusty and me, we were tracking an elk all day when nightfall crept up on us. I built a campfire and settled down, when Dusty began to stir and snort, but all quiet-like. After fifteen years with a horse you learn to read it pretty good, and I knew that sorta noise meant something big was stalking us. I figured it had to be a bear or a mountain lion. I grabbed my rifle and built up the campfire, and brought Dusty in close to me. Both of us were as close to that fire as we could tolerate but whatever it was watching us wouldn't let up or cut us any slack.

"Now, if you recall, in nineteen thirty-four we had a horrible dry spell and all the animals were parched and hungry. Game wasn't as plentiful as it had been in years past. So, depending on your order in the food chain, if you were top dog you were probably starving to death. Well, by dawn both me and Dusty hadn't slept a wink. We were both pretty darned spooked by whatever it was watching us, and we hightailed it out of there. The bad of it is the thing watching us turned out to be *things*, as in a pack of wolves. I don't know if you've ever seen a pack of dogs go on the rampage but, son, let me tell you something. A pack of wolves is one of the scariest sights a human being can ever encounter. So, these wolves come at us from all sides. I don't know if they were rabid or what but they attacked us like we were pieces of raw meat. First they started nipping at Dusty's flanks, then at his throat. It was like they could have cared less I was on his back. They had no fear. Anyway, when they started going for Dusty's throat I pulled out my revolver and fired a couple of quick shots at 'em. Dusty was already spooked and, well, firing that shot so close to his head caused him to spook even more and he reared back and took a tumble. I fell off and he fell on top of my leg. Crushed the knee. I still remember that loud crack. It was a horrible sound. But I was so focused on defending myself from the wolves that my leg didn't even hurt. Not one bit. . . at least until later.

"So, Dusty was on his side with my leg pinned underneath him and the wolves started going for his throat. They knew exactly what to do. My pistol had flown in the air somewhere. Never did find it. The rifle was still strapped in the saddle and loaded. I fired off every round and killed a slew of wolves but there was so many of 'em. So many of 'em. . . ."

The Sheriff paused. Recalling that pivotal moment in time, his hands began to tremble. He licked his lips and started breathing shallow and fast.

". . . *and they killed my horse*." His eyes welled. "Those bastards killed my horse. There was nothing I could do. And Dusty never fought it. He knew. He knew what was going to happen. And he never fought it. He just turned his head to look at me. He turned his head one last time and looked back at me with his eyes wide open. Not frightened. Just knowing. He knew death was upon him. And I think he was more concerned about me than about himself. He made this low growl whinny and laid his head down and let the wolves have at him. It was bad. Really bad."

The Sheriff took a long swig from his iced tea and fell back into his chair. Martha held his hand to keep it from shaking out of control.

"How'd you get out of there alive?" the boy asked.

"To be honest, I don't really know. I'd run out of bullets and I knew those wolves would be coming at me next. I remember grabbing the rifle barrel and getting ready to swing it like a baseball bat to defend myself. But the rest is like a dream. Looking back on it, it's hard for me to know what was real and what wasn't. The doctor said I probably went into shock. That's why my memory is clouded."

Martha squeezed his hand. "Go ahead and tell him, John," she said. "Billy is like family. Tell him what happened next. It's okay."

The Sheriff took a deep breath and looked at the boy and the girl, and then back to the boy. "Well, I don't want you to think I'm crazy or nothing but it was like I just said—sort of like being in a dream. Everything got blurry and slow motion. It's kind of hard to figure out what's real and what isn't but, here it goes. . . As I got ready to swing the rifle, a white stallion came from out of nowhere and charged at those wolves. How he got there beats the heck out of me. And why he defended me, is beyond reason. All I know is that he stomped the ever-loving life out of two or three of 'em and scared the rest away. By now I had collapsed on my back, maybe blacked out, and when I come-to he was sniffing my face and nibbling on me. Without thinking about the fact a wild mustang had just rescued me, I threw my arms around his neck. He didn't like that one bit and jerked back, and in the process pulled me free. I think he knew I didn't mean him any harm. He came back around and stood over me, and stared. It was like he thought I was someone else. Like he was looking for someone else. When he figured out I wasn't the one, he left. Just left me and disappeared back into the trees. As for me, I recovered my senses and worked up a splint for my leg, and hobbled back down the mountain. By now, I was in a lot of pain. Fortunately, Jimmy Porter's place was about two miles below and I made it there, and he hauled me off to the hospital in Billings. They did the best they could with the knee but it got crushed pretty bad."

"Did you ever get another horse?" the girl asked.

"Nope. One good horse is all a man ever needs in a lifetime."

"Did you ever go back to where Dusty fell?" the boy pursued.

"Indeed, I did. I went back there before the snows came. It was mid-September. Went with Martha."

Martha still held his hand and smiled sadly recalling the day. "Yes," she said. "We hiked to the spot. I'm glad it wasn't any further or I don't believe John would have made it there and back."

"But we did it. Didn't we, Martha?"

"Yes. We did. And I'm glad we did for your sake." She turned to the boy and the girl. "I don't believe John could have lived with himself if he hadn't paid Dusty his last respects."

"There couldn't of been much remains left." The boy stated.

"Just bones and his tail and mane."

"Did you keep his mane?" the boy asked.

"Yup. Call me Indian superstitious but, yes, I did. Martha is going to hang it on a tree below the mountain when I die. You know. On the Indian hill with all the horse manes."

"Only if you go first, dear. If I go first, you'd better have a second."

The Sheriff turned to the boy. "If that happens, son, could you do that for me? Hang Dusty's mane on one of those trees? I keep it in the top drawer of my clothes hutch along with a hundred dollars."

"I'd be honored to do it, sir," the boy said, "but I ain't taking the hundred dollars."

Taken aback by the boy's sincerity, the Sheriff thanked him for being such a well-mannered young man.

Later, as Billy was walking out the door to escort Polly back to her 'Aunt Edna's,' Martha made him promise to return for supper the next time he came to town. The boy said he would. She fondly hugged him and kissed him on the cheek. Even rough and gruff Sheriff John Toms gave the boy a hug and wished him well on the next roundup. The two silently waved good-bye until the youngsters had rounded the street corner.

"They make a real smart couple. Don't they, Martha?"

Martha clicked her tongue before answering. "Oh, I don't think so."

"Really? Why not?"

"Oh, John. Do I look like I just fell off the turnip cart?"

"What do you mean, Martha?"

"You know exactly what I mean. We can't have Isaac and Jennie's son dating a common whore. Can we?"

28

Miss Edna's establishment hid from view on the south side of Laurel on a dusty dead-end street fittingly named *Inferno Lane*. The house nestled underneath giant sycamores and elms, surrounded by older homes of lesser stature, shacks and shanties to be exact, that traced their lineage to the 1880s. Edna's always sported a fresh coat of white paint, matching the white picket fence out front and the small sign inscribed 'Aunt Edna's Boarding House.' Some patrons thought the home looked "spiffy as all get-out" for a two-bit house of ill repute. Most never noticed the irony of a prostitution house painted virgin white or smelling of antiseptic.

During the 1920s, Edna did attempt to make a legitimate go of it, providing a bona fide hostel for vagabonds and weary highway travelers. But after two years of struggling through the Great Depression, she converted her humble enterprise into something that could pay the bills. No surprise most respectable people in town knew nothing of their one whorehouse. Local folks had no need for boarding houses and, more importantly, knew that 'One should never venture to south Laurel after dark. That's where the Coloreds live.' Black Americans had long chosen refuge in that notorious corner of town. In fact, most of the folks who lived there derived income working in varying capacities for Miss Edna. Beulah co-hosted the home with Edna and managed the girls, their money and their habits. Jackie contracted the clap and could no longer provide services but could cook up a heck of a good meal to feed the throngs of white men frequenting the joint. Big Mike, a giant of a man, served as bouncer and enforcer and, from time-to-time, protector of whores' civil rights. And there was Edna, a matronly-looking woman sixty years old whose dour white face never hinted of her true lusty nature. Edna's life goal was simple and to the point: make lots of money and move to Florida. Why Edna became obsessed with moving to Florida no one really understood. She had a family stashed in Helena and had never been outside of Montana. Nevertheless, like all aspiring whores (or whores' madams), Edna had dreams and the dreams never involved payoffs and false smiles and staring at the ceiling from her backside or, worse, freezing her exposed tail off in the dead of winter.

For most folks, the town's house of ill repute seemed harmless enough. Miss Edna and the girls provided a service that from the local male perspective was in constant short supply. Edna and her girls were simply angels in disguise. The problem with all this freethinking was that while some townsfolk in Laurel remained steeped in an anything-goes Wild West bygone era, most had evolved with the law-abiding temperament of the twentieth century.

The sunset had already overtaken the boy and the girl when they climbed the front porch stoop to Edna's boarding house. The boy took off his hat and in his customary manner fumbled with its brim. He had kissed just one girl before and that played out long ago in the tenth grade with an equally novice ninth grader. Now, he had fallen in lust with an experienced woman-child. Clearly, Polly portended to be nothing like the freshman. Standing with one foot planted on the stoop and the other foot two steps below, all the boy knew was how much he wanted to kiss the girl.

"I've got to go inside," she said.

Beulah peered through the front door window and flicked the porch light on and off eerily in rhythm to the beat of *Moonlight Serenade* blaring inside.

"Why? Why do you have to go?"

"Because I have to get ready for work. Because they don't like me being late."

"Aw-w-w, come on. You got time. I know you do."

"No. I've got to go," she chided.

It was as though she had changed personalities. He noticed halfway back to Edna's how Polly had broken out in a sweat in the cooler evening air and began shivering and rubbing her arms to stay warm when, in fact, the air felt ideal. He was oblivious to how her body craved heroin and now shivered for a fix.

"But you know I'm sweet on you," he pressed. "I wantta kiss you. *Now.*"

"We can't. Maybe next time you're in town. Okay? Next time, Toots."

"But I've been waiting for this moment my entire life. I want to tell you how much—"

The girl dodged his lips. She lunged for the doorknob.

"But—"

Before he could say *I love you,* she vanished inside the house slamming the door. Beulah greeted her with a readied hypodermic needle.

29

"Congratulations, Mister Bartell, on your kill. I knew you'd come through."

"Well, sir. It is what you hired me for. Killing the bosses, that is." The boy almost choked on the words while spewing the lie. It was the Captain, however, who had insisted on the face-to-face meeting and the commendation. How could he admit the truth to the Captain? Yet, sitting in the dank study on the worn Victorian couch for the second time in less than two weeks, the boy felt more confident in conversing with his mysterious employer. The lie fed the confidence. The confidence stoked the lie.

Fumbling with his hat, the boy recalled the memory of the strange odor permeating the room. As he suspected before, the recollection traced to the night the deputies brought the cleric's body to the funeral home. The defrocked priest had stuck a shotgun in his mouth after consuming a bottle of Irish whiskey. Little remained of the priest's head but the body had still managed to convulse up bile and whiskey. As with most violent deaths, the priest had defecated. All this alchemy had mixed with blood in the body bag for two days in the summer heat. When Henry unzipped the bag, he nearly passed out; he delegated to the boy the task of heaving the corpse onto the slab. The Captain's study reeked of the same sickening smell of death. The boy looked to his left and back to the hallway from where he thought the odor emanated, where Lieutenant Mullin stood at attention like a posed mannequin soldier. He turned toward the desk and sniffed the air. Captain Belial had scooted all the way forward and the boy could now see the man's hideous face in its entirety: the scars and the huge dimpled indentation on the forehead, the lifeless and black sunken eyes and the yellowed burnt skin awash in caustic ointment still needed years after the mustard gas explosion. Yes. It was the combination of rotting skin and fresh ointment permeating the room. This time the Captain felt bold enough to expose his shredded face in the light and let the boy see the toll taken during the Great War. The portions of the Captain's face not disfigured by the tragedy were the chin and mouth, and the mouth bore an unequivocal sneer, perhaps more hideous than the rest of the face. The sneer appeared quite pleased with itself, the boy, and the revelation of how the newly found science of rounding up wild mustangs had worked beyond expectation. Just five herds remained. With a bit of divine providence, the crew would be moving onto Oregon by the end of August. They could lay to rest twenty years of laboring at Pryor Mountain. Indeed, the Captain seemed pleased as a Cheshire cat that had just caught a mouse.

The boy watched the Captain swivel in the chair, pour a brandy and settle back into the shadow. Sully and Bob warned him that no one other than Lieutenant Mullin had ever seen the Captain more than once. "Kid," they said, "your shit must not stink if the man wants to see you again," The truth of the matter was one other cowboy had visited the Captain not twice but three times.

"If you don't mind me asking, sir, there's something I'm a curious about," the boy threw out.

"And what is that, son?"

"Who is Dante Alegre?"

Lieutenant Mullin stirred from his pose. The Captain moved back into the light.

"*Who?*"

"Dante Alegre. His name is penciled on one of the timbers out front. On the entrance."

"I can answer that," the Lieutenant responded. "He was a young drover like yourself. He didn't like what we do to the mustangs and he quit. Collected his pay and took off."

The story did not exactly jibe with what the cowboys had stated.

"It is like I told you before," the Captain interjected, "when we make a pact, I expect you to live up to your end. I always live up to mine. Always. If you violate the pact, then woe be unto you."

"How do you mean that, sir?"

"I mean if you violate our pact you can no longer be part of this fold. Plain and simple."

The boy was about to ask what the Captain meant by 'this fold' when the Lieutenant spoke up again in an obvious attempt to change the subject.

"It seems we have some trouble brewing on the horizon. Isn't that right Captain?"

The Captain nodded his head. "Yes, we do. There is a herd escaping north. I believe you and our half-breed spotted it ten miles on the other side of the mountain."

"Yes, sir. About one-fifty of 'em."

"Well, here is the challenge for us, son. We cannot let that herd move beyond Stratford Mountain. If they do, they will move onto Crow reservation land and we are not permitted in there. It is imperative that we round up all the herds by summer's end, this herd included. The mountain must be totally eradicated of all mustangs."

"Well, sir, seems to me there's no way we can stop 'em. I mean, by the time we all mount up and ride up there it'll be too late. They're too far away and moving too fast."

"My thoughts exactly. But here's the rub. We have technology on our side."

The boy thought for a few seconds before responding. "*The airplane*."

"Yes."

"But the airplane can only carry two or three of us and no horses. How we gonna roundup mustangs on foot?"

"I only need one of you to stop the herd."

"Only one?"

"Yes, son. That *one* is you. Remember what I told you the first day you stepped in here. I said, 'Rid the herd of their leadership and the herd becomes easier to deceive and manipulate.' If we stop the herd's leader, the white horse known by the Indians as Remliel, the herd will flounder. It is my belief the white stallion is the one leading them north. Kill him and they will return south to Pryor Mountain on their own. They will follow their mating instincts, which this time of year always brings them back to their stomping grounds."

"So you want me to shoot him?"

"Exactly. Our half-breed will scout for you. You two make a good team. I have T.F. lined up to take you both there in the morning. He'll wait for you on the ground until the job is done. Are you up for it, son?"

The boy looked at the Captain and then at the Lieutenant and then back to the Captain who was now wearing another contemptuous sneer.

"Guess I don't really got a choice in the matter now, do I? Don't wantta break our pact."

"You always have a choice, son. You're an adult."

The boy thought about rehashing the unfinished business concerning Dante Alegre but decided it best to remain silent for the time being. "Fine. Tell T.F. that Hayyel and I'll be ready at sunrise."

"Excellent. I knew I could count on you to do my bidding."

XXX

I was eight years old when my Pa took me to the shooting range for the very first time. Of course Pa was my instructor and a good-un he was. Looking back I think he kinda felt sorry for me. That's probably what spurred him into getting me out of the house. I had few friends. No mother. A teenage brother more interested in the opposite sex than taking an interest in a baby brother. And my Pa was busy doing funeral business work six days a week. So I got ignored. Got lonely. I guess you could say I was one of those lost kids who fell through the cracks. That's why Sunday afternoons became real important to me. It was my time to hang out with my Pa. That's when we went to the shooting range. Sundays. And my Pa would talk to me. Mostly about how to properly handle a rifle. Sometimes about other things. Like about Ma and him. And about what's important in life. And whatnot.

I do remember all of that. Like it was yesterday. Pa brought me in and introduced me to his buddies. They was all pretty good shots but mostly town folk. Not farmers or ranchers or real hunters. A lot different how good a shot you were if you had to put food on the table. Anyways. Pa had me kneel down and use my free knee to steady the rifle. What's called a three-position. I remember him whispering in my right ear and telling me how to fit the bull's-eye in the sight. Carry my elbows. Read the wind. Squeeze the trigger without jerking the rifle about. And I did exactly what he told me to do. What Pa said I needed to do in order to make a clean shot. And the last thing he'd always say to me before I fired. "Always aim straight and true. Never rush the moment. When you're finished, savor what you've done."

Now in those days we mostly used a five-ring target with a four-inch black bull's-eye. We'd shoot at fifty yards. Without a scope. Only used iron sights. That's just the way it was done. The old-timers' ways. And I squeezed off that first round and Pa laughed to beat the band. "What's so funny, Pa?" I remember asking to which he says, "I think you missed the entire target. It's okay."

"No, sir. I believe I just put five shots through the center. Did exactly what you told me to do. Your eyes must be bad."

Pa got the funniest look on his face. And he walked to the target and he yanked the paper down and brought it back giggling like a school kid. "Billy, I do believe I owe you an apology," he says. "I don't know how you did it, but you just made a perfect score fresh outa the chute. I am very proud of you."

By now a group of his buddies had gathered around and they was patting my Pa on the back telling him what I did was amazing. They nicknamed me 'Billy-the-Kid' on account I was good with that rifle. Called me a prodigy or something like that. They asked me to repeat my feat and I tried but couldn't do what I did before. Now this upset my Pa. One minute he was the man-of-the-hour and the next the father of a runny-nose scrawny little kid who couldn't shoot straight. "What happened, Billy?" he asked me. And I says, "You're not whispering in my ear and telling me what to do. That's what's happened. I need you to whisper in my ear."

So my Pa got down on his knees again and talked softly into that right ear of mine and I got off five steady shots all in the bull's-eye. And he laughed and pinched my nose. "Guess we're a team, you and me," he said. And we were. Even when I got a little older we'd start off a competition with him kneeling next to me and whispering in my ear and giving me words to live by.

For a year after my Pa died I avoided going to the shooting range. Too many memories. One day Henry says to me, "Hey, Squirt, let's you and me go to the range. Some of Pa's friends called on the phone. They say they miss your ugly mug." So we went and I tried to get back in the hang of things but couldn't. Henry saw how frustrated I was and he asks me what's wrong with 'Billy-the-Kid' to which I said, "Without Pa whispering in my ear I can't do anything right." Well now. Henry yanks me aside and gets all stern and father-like himself. He says to me, "You little brat. Don't you know nothin'? Pa's always with you. Always will be. When you stop believing he ain't, that's when you're in trouble. Quit feeling sorry for yourself. Let Pa back in. Let him whisper in that ear of yours and get on with your life. All you gotta do is listen."

And I took Henry's advice. I suppose big brothers are good for a thing or two cuz from that moment on I did my best to listen for Pa's whispers. And guess what? The more I let him in the clearer his words became. 'Always aim straight and true. Never rush the moment. When you're finished, savor what you've done.'

31

The Staggerwing soared north of Pryor Mountain to the spot where the mustangs had been sighted a week before. It took a bearing north-northeast toward the Crow reservation where the horses were thought to be roaming. When T.F. got within a mile of the reservation boundary, Hayyel spotted the herd pushing through the trees and toward an expansive foothill void of most vegetation. Even at the lower elevation, a thick cap of summer snow clung to the hill's crest before cascading into a canyon and a raging creek lined with juniper. The Crow scout pointed to the ground and the horses for the boy's perusal. The boy peered over the front of the lower wing and motioned he could see the herd, too. For five minutes T.F. had been revving the engine, making verbal communication almost impossible. Thermals off the plains to the north had been bucking the low flying craft about. Without the additional rpm's they would have to fly at a higher altitude or move in a different direction. Hayyel tapped T.F. on the shoulder signaling he spotted the herd. Finding a suitable landing patch now played in the hands of the pilot.

They had been in the air less than forty-five minutes and the excitement of viewing the earth from a bird's view had already lost its novelty, at least for the boy. The rush from the first experience had come and gone. This second flight settled into a far less thrilling routine. Maybe it was the reality that the plane had become just another extension of the PMRC killing machine, or the idea that something so technologically wonderful turned into so diabolically evil. Either way, the boy no longer delighted at soaring high above the trees and canyons. He took no pleasure in the grandeur of the landscape off the wingtips. His beautiful Montana had become less beautiful.

In a way, blocking out feelings of pleasure had always been the boy's defensive mechanism. Coping with guilt and the grim prospect of death had always left him numb. He summoned the same mechanism to deal with the bodies at the funeral home. And, just like the funeral business, what began as youthful curiosity yielded to disdain.

As he stared through the craft's window at the horses scattering from the roar of the engine, one thought preoccupied his mind: he alone stood between the herd's survival and their death. The very notion skewed his face in torment. Even his hands quaked over the revelation, but no one would have noticed. Each passenger was there for a reason. Each passenger stewed preoccupied in his own role with the dark task.

A few minutes later, T.F. broke the pattern of hand signals, hollering back that he couldn't find a safe place to land. He was flying north into Crow country. Hayyel asked him to follow a creek tributary east. The plane banked and swooped to a lower altitude. T.F. throttled the engine back as the air turbulence lessened. Hayyel tapped the boy and announced they were flying over his winter cabin.

The boy spoke, a first since takeoff. "I thought you lived with the rest of 'em at Crow Agency."

Hayyel explained how he preferred being in the wilderness alone. When late September arrived, he would hole up at the cabin through spring, trapping game and consuming canned goods hauled in by packhorse. "I keep many provisions in case snows lock me in."

"How do you do to keep from going crazy?" the boy pursued.

"Read. I read books. Mostly classics. And I fish a lot."

As he spoke, the plane reversed course and swooped even lower over the cabin. This time the boy got a better feel for their bearings relative to Pryor Mountain.

T.F. zoomed above the herd again but this time out of the east. He banked the craft around two short ridges and then dived into a gray gypsum caldron. Except for a few lone sages, the bleak landing site resembled how the boy imagined a lunar landscape to look. The Beechcraft touched down safely without bouncing. Its tires sank into the soft moist gypsum. The propeller kicked up little dust and any hint of their presence went unnoticed by the herd. T.F. bragged on his landing skill and goaded the boy, asking who the best pilot in the world was. The boy responded, "Beats me." T.F. thumbed his chest and bragged, "You're looking at him, kid."

Once they taxied to a stop, both the boy and Hayyel figured they had an easy hike to intercept the mustangs. Because the morning was still young, all agreed the job should complete by midday before the heat had the chance to set in and the sun bake their necks. For speed's sake, they didn't lug the walkie-talkie. This would be a surgical strike. T.F. would wait in the airplane and if the hunters failed to return by noon, he would come looking for them from the air. T.F. said he had a copy of *Gone with the Wind* that would keep him occupied for at least five hours. Rhett Butler had just ridden his steed to Scarlet O'Hara's rescue and he expected the two lovers to get married within another chapter or two. Neither the boy nor Hayyel had a clue about what the man had just said.

32

Hayyel led the way over the first gypsum hill before scaling down a mudded cliff on the far side and into a shallow ravine. The boy followed with the rifle strapped over his shoulder. His cowboy hat dangled over his back and swung back-and-forth by the drawstring strung about his neck. Through it all, the Indian scout remained silent. The boy knew Hayyel had doubts as to his resolve to put down the boss horse. As they scaled the far side of the ravine and ascended the second hill, the boy casually mentioned his own encounter with a white horse seven years earlier when he was a child of ten.

"Do you think it's the same white horse we're going after?" the boy asked.

"Yes."

"Why do you think that?"

"Because these things always come full circle. Maybe you were meant to kill the horse seven years ago and you did not. Now you must. You must kill it and not think twice on it. Now, be quiet. You think too much. Too much thinking is not good for any human being."

The boy cracked a smile. "You just called me a human being."

"Even I make mistakes, *boy*. When the white horse dies, when you cut off its mane, then you will be a human being. You must do what is expected of you. Do you understand?"

"I understand. I need to shoot the horse. Cut off its mane."

"Yes. Now be quiet."

They descended the second hill into a grassy coulee and climbed to the top where it broke into the gorge and the creek raged fresh with snow runoff. Hayyel looked for a way across but the torrent proved impassible. He yanked the boy behind a juniper and pointed to the snow ridge twelve hundred feet away. The boy looked downstream and up to where the snow joined the raging water. The white horse gazed across the chasm to the Crow reservation. All the horse understood was that safety lay on the other side. Getting through the raging water posed an obstacle.

"You need to take the shot now," Hayyel announced. "You will not get any closer to the white horse. He is too clever. He is *izaquabak*."

The boy slid the rifle off his shoulder, disengaged the safety and fell to one knee. The air in the gorge hung thick and misty but also calm. He knew that from twelve hundred feet and angled upward twenty degrees, the bullet's slug would fall less than six inches. It would be an easy shot. He peeped through the aperture and made adjustments, telling himself the entire time how the horse was just another target. He needed to concentrate on the target. Yet, as he wrapped his finger around the trigger, he hesitated. The white horse turned to look at him. It was as though the horse knew the boy hid behind the juniper.

"You have to do this," Hayyel blurted out. "You are the only one. You have to."

"But why?"

Hayyel knelt behind the boy and placed his hand on the boy's shoulder, whispering in the boy's ear. "Because all this ends with you. All this begins with you."

The boy's eyes began to water. He wiped back tears, took a deep breath and aimed. Then, he squeezed the trigger and watched the outcome.

The horse took the full brunt of the impact without wavering. It stepped back and fell on a front knee, and tumbled sideways and slid down the incline into the water leaving a trail of blood on the snow.

When they rose to peer down the gorge, neither the boy nor the scout could see the horse. The water had washed its body downstream. Except for the trail of blood, the creature had vanished as if it never existed.

"Do we need to make sure its dead?" the boy asked.

"No. Your job is done. You have done well."

When they returned to the Beechcraft, T.F. was upset because he didn't have enough time to get to the good parts of his book. The boy said nothing and collapsed curled up in the backseat of the craft. Hayyel stated dryly that the world's greatest pilot needed to get them the hell out of there.

The mood in the bunkhouse was just as somber. Sully and Bob had propped their boots tall on the pine table. Both cowboys were leaning back on their chairs smoking pipes and listening to a radio broadcast. Neither looked up at Hayyel or the boy when they walked in or asked if the boy had succeeded in killing the white horse.

"What is wrong?" Hayyel asked.

"Listen," Sully said, pointing to the radio.

A man was speaking. His voice reverberated over what sounded like a PA system. The voice paused choked-up before starting again. *"Today I consider myself the luckiest man. . . ."*

"Who is it?" the boy asked.

"It's Lou Gehrig," Bob answered. He turned to face Hayyel. Tears streaked down his cheeks. "He can't play baseball no more. He's dyin'. Tell you one damned thing—this old world of ours has turned upside down."

"It's the saddest day of my life," Sully added. "What are we gonna do without the likes of Lou Gehrig? Can you imagine? An American institution like that dyin' off?"

The boy said not a word. He walked straight to his bunk and lay down. A few seconds later, he lit a cigarette and stared at the ceiling.

33

The '36 Ford Flatbed bounced through the sharp turn on the dirt switchback nearly throwing its two platform passengers over the side for the tenth time. Sully turned around to check and see if they were still hanging on. He rapped the rear window. "Hey, kid, you and the girl still doin' okay?" The back of the boy's head nodded 'yes.' The girl's head lay snug against the boy's shoulder. "Like I told you earlier, you both can sit up here next to Bob. The Chief and me, we'll come back there. No need for that purdy little thing to get all dusty and bounced about."

"We're fine," the boy hollered back through the glass. "Really."

Hayyel leaned over and whispered to Sully, "I think the boy wants privacy." He glanced over at Bob. "And Bob, he smells too much for the girl."

"Hard not to work up a stink tacklin' the Bighorn Mountains in this old jalopy. If you all don't think so, just give it a go," Bob fired back.

Both men shook their heads 'no thanks.' Both knew the new road exceeded their driving talents.

It had been over four weeks since the boy hunted down the white horse. Since then, three herds had been rounded up and three more boss stallions shot by the boy. One herd remained on top of the mountain. The other herd, the one that almost escaped onto the Crow reservation, they spotted at the mountain base ascending the northeastern face en route for a return to the top. The airplane and walkie-talkies proved invaluable. Roundups accomplished at record pace. And Hayyel predicted the last two herds would be captured by early August. The revelation provided cause for celebration and Captain Belial gave the cowboys four days off with pay.

All along, it had been Sully's idea to travel to Sheridan for the annual rodeo. In past years, he never would have given it a thought but with the newly finished WPA road over the Bighorns, what used to take twelve hours in a long swing around the mountain chain now drove in four. The problem with the new road, however, was the five-mile stretch over the mountain's crest; it remained unpaved and potholed switchbacks beat up drivers. "This damned road would've been a lot easier to tackle on a horse," Bob complained every other minute. As for the boy and girl, they didn't care if the trip took four hours or four days. They had been lost in each other's company since Laurel. Moreover, the boy had yet to consummate the relationship. He felt certain two nights alone with Polly at the Pine Lodge Motel would seal the deal, but at a price. Because the nights fell on a Friday and Saturday, working girl nights, permission was sought from Miss Edna. Tipping the woman a $50 incentive didn't hurt. The boy just hoped the 'tip' money would prove justifiable.

What spurred the initial interest in the rodeo was the potential of prize winnings. Sully read that the rodeo agency brought in "*some of the meanest plumb-loco mustangs ever lassoed.*" At least that is what it said word-for-word in the newspaper advertisement. The cowboy who could break his assigned mustang in the quickest time would win a $900 cash prize.

"Hell," Sully bragged, "those boys oughtta just give it to me now. Nobody up in these parts got an edge on a Texas cowboy, anyways."

"That's for damned sure," Bob threw in.

When they rumbled into town, all five went straight to the arena. The events had already started. No one thought the trip over the Bighorns would take as long as it did. Both cowboys signed up and paid their $1 entry fee. Hayyel refused to add his name to the list, stating how breaking wild horses was for fools, queers, and Texans. With the peer pressure, the boy felt obliged to sign up and kicked in his dollar.

The competition involved a cowboy-contestant turned loose in the grand arena along with a wild mustang as two thousand people looked on and cheered (or jeered, depending upon one's perspective). The contestant had to saddle the horse and ride it until the horse displayed a sense of rein control, timed from the start to a buck-*less* finish. The contestant with the shortest time would win the $900 prize. For the sake of expediency, all horses released into the arena had been pre-bridled with bosal hackamores, the long rope reins draped about the horses' necks. First order of business entailed saddling; second, mounting; and third, the ride itself. If the contestant managed to mount, the horse would inevitably buck him off to the dusty arena floor. Since 1931, no one had ever succeeded in winning the grand prize money of $100. Hence, the cumulative purse of $900.

That particular evening just seven contestants were foolhardy enough to attempt to break the corralled and angry mustangs. The first horse, the one named *Killer-Diller*, epitomized why, after eight years of failure, a mere seven cowboys were willing to give it a try. Cowboy number one, a bowlegged drunk named Roy, hailed from Casper's Bar Nunn Ranch. While his equally drunk and rowdy friends cheered him on, Roy staggered-up to the horse with the saddle in both arms and plopped it on the horse's back. As he bent down to cinch it tight, the horse spun right and kicked Roy in the head. Roy stumbled back and keeled over. No one in the audience knew for sure if the old cowboy got knocked out or passed out. Either way, everyone found it hilarious and, like Romans in the Coliseum, hollered for the next cowboy-gladiator while two officials dragged Roy away by his boots to an awaiting doctor.

The next horse had no specific name but went by the nickname *Skittish*. Every time his rider tried to get close with the saddle, the horse inched away. After ten minutes of failures, the cowboy threw down the saddle and chased after the horse. The spectators cheered and laughed, but mostly laughed. Fifteen minutes later, everyone understood the meaning of the mustang's nickname and gave it a standing ovation. The cowboy inevitably gave up and kicked the saddle for good measure.

Three more cowboys tried and failed, including Bob. None of the three ever came close to saddling their respective mustangs.

Sully had a more novel approach. He placed the saddle on the arena floor and started yelling obscenities at his mustang, the red dun stallion *Angry Thinker*. The tactic worked. The animal's ears perked while the rest of its carcass froze spellbound with curiosity. Realizing that he had somehow captured the horse's attention, Sully walked straight to the animal and socked it in the side of the head with his fist. *Wham*. The horse stumbled sideways and shook itself sober from the heavy-handed punch. That's when Sully retrieved the saddle, threw it over the horse, cinched it tight and climbed aboard. "Nothin' to this, Compadre," he yelled to Bob who was sitting on a fence rail. He then heeled the horse in the flanks and yanked the hackamore's reins left. The infuriated mustang jumped three feet off the ground with all fours, came down twisting right and bucked Sully left to the ground. The Texas cowboy saw stars once he hit dust. Everyone roared in delight.

"Your turn, boy." Hayyel stated matter-of-factly.

"Shoot. I don't know anything about breaking wild mustangs. They look meaner than all get out."

"Few white men do understand horses. You will not be the first."

"Well, how am I gonna do any better than those cowboys?"

"Simple. Take your time. Do not look the horse in the eyes. Do not walk straight to it. Walk sideways. When you touch it, stroke its face and eyes gently. Then, talk soft to it."

"What do I say to a horse?"

"Tell it you are its friend. Tell it you will protect it. Tell it you are sorry for killing the white horse. If it believes you, it will let you ride."

The boy was too apprehensive not to take Hayyel's advice.

Now, cowboys and cowgirls, our last contestant of the evening is a young man from Billings, Montana. He's never tried to break a wild mustang before. He's new at it. So, let's cheer him on in good old Wyoming style. Let's hear it for seventeen-year-old Billy Bartell. . . .

The girl stuck her pinkie fingers in the corners of her mouth and whistled a shrill 'go-get-em Billy.' Everyone cheered. Sully walked past the boy dusting off his jeans. "Kid, I hope you do a hell of a lot better than me. Make us proud."

...And let's give a round of applause for our Pryor Mountain mustang, a scrappy two-year-old colt named Son-of-a-Gun.

A potbellied official hat-swatted the mustang into the center of the arena. The boy stopped dead in his tracks. The horse bore identical markings to the white horse, Remliel. He looked back at Hayyel who shrugged his shoulders in disbelief. "It is a coincidence," Hayyel shouted. "Could be his offspring. Maybe."

The boy laid down the saddle and stood for minutes observing the horse's behavior. The horse's ears flipped back; it breathed in quick shallow pants and shivered uncontrollably. The poor thing needed water. The boy shuffled toward it at an angle while avoiding eye contact. When the boy got within ten feet, the horse began to pivot. That's when the boy stopped moving and spoke to it in a calm soothing tone. "You don't know me," he said, "but I know you. And I won't hurt you. You're a good fella. You're just scared. You're scared of all these people. Tell you what. You let me ride you and I'll make sure nobody ever hurts you again. Okay, fella?"

The boy's voice played to the horse's instincts. The horse turned around with its ears now perked forward to listen. The boy crept closer and kept repeating the same words. The bridle's rope rein dangled and the boy backed up to it and gathered it in his hand, the whole time looking at the ground. "There," he whispered, "that wasn't so hard. Was it? Sooner or later we all get roped in." He glanced over to the girl who was staring at him frightened but smiling. Sully leaned against the railing holding his hat as though in prayer and talking to himself. Hayyel gave him a thumbs-up and Bob hollered out, "You can do it, kid. Hang in there."

Wanting some action or blood or both, the audience grew impatient and a few hecklers shouted disparaging words like "hurry up" and "get on him, slow-poke," but for the most part, the boy ignored their rants and continued at his own speed. He backed closer to the horse's head and held out a hand palm-up. The horse sniffed it, scouring for scent. The boy remembered the rock candies stashed in his jeans pocket and retrieved one and placed it in the outreached hand. A few seconds later, the horse had consumed the sweet morsel and wanted more. The boy fed the horse the next four pieces one at a time. Then, he slowly pivoted on his feet and faced the horse. The gangly colt ignored his repositioning and riffled his shirt and pants looking for more candy. "Sorry, fella. I ain't got any of the good stuff left. Tell you what. You let me on top and I'll buy you your own bagful of candies."

He tucked up the rope, looped it around the horse's neck and fastened the loose end under the bridle. Once the loop closed, he slid a hand to the bottom of the hackamore to steady his grip and with the other hand placed it against the horse's muzzle while the horse attempted to nibble on invisible candy. He ran his hand up the horse's nose and stroked the area between the eyes and on the cheeks and the neck and the ears. When he finally did make eye contact, he told the young colt everything else that needed to be said to put it at ease and to ease his own conscience. "I knew your daddy. And I killed him. I wish I hadn't. But I did. And if I could take it all back, I would. But I can't. It was the worst thing I ever did. Worst thing. And I am so sorry. I won't let anybody hurt you. I promise. You've gotta trust me one hundred per cent on this. Trust me, fella. Please."

He led the horse to the saddle and laid the gear on its back. He cinched the saddle's strap under the horse and then slid his boot in the stirrup and swung his other leg over. The colt turned around to look at him and the boy smiled and stroked its neck. "Let's go, fella," he said. "Let's show 'em what a Montana mustang is made outta." He gently heeled the horse in the flanks and the horse slow-trotted forward. He pulled the rein left and the horse followed his lead. He pulled it right and the horse followed right. For the next five minutes the horse and rider paraded around the arena left and right, stopping and twirling, all to the applause of Sheridan, Wyoming.

When he dismounted, the same official, the portly pasty-faced man walked up to the boy and shook his hand. The man carried a megaphone and announced to the audience that Billy Bartell of Billings, Montana, had just won $900 and the once-wild untamed mustang colt named Son-of-a-Gun. "What are you going to do with all this money, son?" the man asked, craning his lips through the megaphone.

"Well, sir, I'm gonna give it to my girlfriend. It and the other money I got saved up for her," the boy answered. "The money is gonna take her to Hollywood. She's gonna become a famous movie star."

Polly ran into the arena jumping up-and-down. She threw her arms around the boy. "What a wonderful present," she said. "I love you, Billy Bartell. I love you."

34

The boy and his entourage took the mustang to one of the empty rodeo stalls for feed and water. A few minutes later, the same awards official and three other well-dressed cowboys, all clean-shaven and dapper with fresh bandanas, confronted him and the PMRC crew. "Say," the man said, "aren't you the cowboys that capture and render mustangs on Pryor Mountain?"

"Yes, sir." The boy answered, more as an apology.

"That's what we thought. Tell you what. We don't like your kind here and don't want you to ever come back. What you're doing to those wild horses is just plain wrong. And we'd like to take our money back, too, but we won't. You won it fair and square. One thing we're not going to let you take, however, is that mustang. We're not going to let you turn him into dog food."

"I wasn't gonna do that, sir. I was gonna release him back where he come from."

"So you can hunt him down again? There's no way we're going to let you leave here tonight with that horse. No way."

One of the other men stepped up and tried yanking the reins out of the boy's hands. The boy refused to yield. Sully glanced over at Bob who was scowling. Bob had already taken their penny out of his shirt pocket to flip it. "Your call," he said. Sully called 'tails' and won the toss, then spun around and jumped in between the boy and the man, shoving the man back.

"You get your little Mormon hands off the boy or I'll break your little Mormon nose."

The man stepped back wide-eyed. "How would you know I'm a Mormon?"

"I know all your well-scrubbed little faces. My partner and I buried two of you down Texas-way. I know all about your kind." He spat some chaw on the cowboy's boots. "If the boy says he's ain't gonna hurt the horse, he ain't gonna hurt it. He's a cut above everyone here. You got it, Bub? He's a cut above."

During the commotion, Billy had pulled himself up on the horse bareback. Using the hackamore, he twirled the horse around. "I'm going back up the way I got here. Up Bighorn pass," he announced. "And I'm riding this mustang all the way to Pryor Mountain. Anyone think they can stop me, good luck trying." He turned to his partners. "I'll see you boys in three days." He winked to Polly and then heeled the horse and galloped out the rodeo grounds and into the darkness.

The boy followed the road over the mountain and the horse ate and drank along the way. When Polly and the crew caught up to him the next day, he was already a quarter of the way home. They bought some food and beverages and ate with him picnic-style on a scenic turnout overlooking the Bighorn basin. While it was one thing to haul dead horses on the flatbed two-at-a-time, it was impossible to prop one live standing horse on top. Everyone knew this, so no one offered to lend a hand. Instead, they gave Billy provisions to make it back and wished him well on returning his horse to the wilds. Polly kissed him long and hard on the lips.

By the morning of the third day, the boy and the colt named Son-of-a-Gun reached the base of Pryor Mountain. From their foothill vantage, they spotted a herd in the distance, the last bunch ascending the mountain to the great meadow high above. The boy dismounted and removed the hackamore and tossed it to the ground. "Well, fella, you won't be needing this anymore. Now, you gotta go that-a-way and I got a go this-a-way," he said pointing out their respective directions. "With a little quick hoofin', I'll be back at camp this evening and you'll be sniffing on some sweet filly." He stroked the horse's face and then swatted its flanks with his hat. The horse took off in a gallop toward the herd. "Don't say thank-you or nothing," he yelled after it. But in his heart he knew the horse truly appreciated everything he had done.

35

The boy couldn't sleep. Neither could Sully. Bob had been snoring for over twenty minutes and Hayyel slept wheezing the way he always did a few seconds after passing out.

"Sully, you still awake?" Sully reached up and pushed the bottom of the boy's bunk mattress. The boy smiled. "I thought so," he said. He rolled over on his back and hesitated a few seconds before asking what had been on his mind since returning by foot to the bunkhouse. "Do you think I did the right thing with Son-of-a-Gun? Turning him loose? I mean, those men, they might've had a point. Why release him if he's just gonna get caught and killed?"

Sully mulled on the question. "Tell you what, kid. If we end up capturing that colt of yours, I will personally run him back up the gap and away from this godforsaken place."

"Good. I promised him—"

"I know, kid. You don't have to spell it out."

"Thanks."

The boy had been staring at the ceiling. The only light in the bunkhouse came from a yellow incandescent porch light swarmed by moths. The ceiling beams shimmered from the moths' shadows and added to the boy's case of insomnia. "I got another question," he posed.

"I'm all ears."

"Back in Sheridan you said you and Bob had buried two Mormons. What hap—"

"What happened? Tell you what happened. Bob got in a fight over a woman. A Mormon woman named Jolene. Well, her brothers found out old Bob wasn't of the same faith and got angry as stirred-up hornets."

"And what faith might Bob be?"

Sully chuckled. "The faith a no faith. Bob don't believe in jack shit. Truth of the matter, Bob's second wife, Lenora, had up and left him for another man. She took their little girl and split. Bob, he got real lonely-like and fell in love on the rebound with this sweet little Mormon girl—"

"How little?"

"Well, I'd venture to say she was fourteen."

The boy tried to hold back on the laughter. "And how old was Bob at the time?"

"Shoot. That was fifteen years ago, so I'd say twenty-six, seven, somethin' like that. Anyways, when the girl's brothers found out about her sneakin' out at night and cavortin' with Bob, they got madder'n hell and came after him." Sully paused to recall the night in question. "Tell you one thing—you don't wantta mess with Bob. And you sure as shootin' don't wantta make him angry. He killed both those boys with his bare hands."

"Didn't the law come after him?"

"Nope. Bob come to me and I helped him bury those two back in the woods where no one could find 'em. No bodies, no murder. Sabe?"

"Yes, sir."

"So, getting back to the story, a few days later this man shows up at my cabin outside Stephenville. Bob had moved in with me and no one knew that except Bob and me. Well, this man knew it, too. And he knocks at the door and he says, 'I have a proposition for you two gentlemen.' He says those words in one of those high-falutin' British kinda accents. And I says back to him, 'What in the devil you talkin' about, mister?' And the man looks me in the eyes with those black eyes of his and says 'I'm talking about the Lord's commandment you broke.' Upon hearing all this Bob yells out, 'Hell, we broke 'em all. Which one?' And the man says, 'Thou shall not murder.' That spooked the you-know-what out of us both. How this complete stranger knew what Bob had done was beyond belief. And about us buryin' the two boys in the woods was downright spooky. So, naturally being the curious individual I am, I invited the man inside my cabin to hear more of what he had to say. Know who that man was?"

Without a hint of hesitation, the boy answered, "Captain Belial."

"You are a smart, kid, ain't you? That's right. Old Captain Belial it was. And the Captain tells us that he's looking for two experienced drovers to help him up Montana-way to round up wild mustangs. Actually, to use his words he said he was 'looking for someone to do his bidding.' Said he had trouble keeping good men. And if we helped him kill off the horses, he'd make sure our souls would be spared the fires of hell and pay us well to boot. Well, naturally, Bob and I thought the man crazy as a loon. And old Bob, he don't believe in heaven or hell, anyways. Just poontang and beer. The kind good money can buy."

"So, why'd you come all the way up here?"

"To get away from the law... and, well, for the money. Funny thing is somehow we always end up spending the money on good times. Still don't got two pennies to rub together."

"And you don't think Captain Belial is the devil or nothing like that?"

"I do. Bob don't. Far as that goes, I'd rather be safe than sorry. Don't wantta spend eternity in hell. Know what I mean?"

"Sure do. You wantta have all the bases covered."

"Amen, brother. So, you got anymore questions for me or can I go to sleep now?"

The boy thought for a few seconds. "Yeah. I got another question."

Sully chuckled. "Well let's just see if old Cowboy Freud can answer it."

"It's about Polly."

"Knew it would be."

"Do you think I shoulda given her all that money?"

Sully mulled on the question. "That's a tough one, kid. Even for an experienced psychiatrist like me." He kept quiet for what seemed like minutes, and then finally spoke up. "Here's what I think: once a whore, always a whore. I know you're sweet on that little girl but it's kinda like her bein' a zebra. She ain't gonna change her stripes. Just not possible for someone like her to change. I believe, when all is said and done, she's gonna break your heart and waste the money you gave her."

"So you're saying I shouldn't a given her the money."

"Nope. That's ain't what I'm sayin'. Given her the money, even if there was only a one in a million chance she'd do good by you, is all you coulda done. Everyone deserves a break, even if it's a long shot. Even if it's a whore."

"Glad you feel that way."

"And I'll tell you one other thing, kid. You can't take it with you. Can you?"

"You mean, you can't take money with you after you die?"

"That's what I mean."

"No, sir. I guess you can't."

"So, when you add everything up, looks like you did the right thing. And I respect that. . . Goodnight, kid."

"Goodnight, Sully."

36

They landed on the ridge below Penn's cabin and hiked to where the most expansive meadow on Pryor Mountain disappeared into a stand of trees. Around the bend of the stand, to the east, lay the highest elevation watering hole and the last herd remaining on the mountain. The other herd, the herd once led by the white horse, was ascending the rugged terrain two thousand feet below the aircraft and spread out for a quarter of a mile eating on the crawl. The herd on top, however, was the one they had come for. Ranked the least dominant of all the herds with an inferior bloodline of mixed ancestry, these mustangs stood smaller and more wiry than their Spaniard cousins.

The boy and Hayyel climbed the crest to the abandoned cabin with the boy lugging the walkie-talkie. There, the two would rest and collect their composure before hiking the half-mile distance to the watering hole. Based on what they sighted out the Beechcraft windows, all of the one hundred and forty-plus mustangs they intended to capture had gathered as a unit around the pooled water. From the air the horses appeared content, observing the bruised sunrise and waiting for the day to unfold. Perhaps the horses knew summer solstice had passed six weeks earlier and their days on the mountain were numbered. Paying homage to the warmth of the sun played to their instincts. More likely, the horses missed the companionship or rivalry of the more dominant herds that were nowhere to be found. After all, this inferior bunch was drinking water at daybreak when, given the natural pecking order of Pryor herds, they normally would wait until midday. Thus, they did not understand the changes. They sensed something afoul and cried out to their missing cousins, baying and wailing while the sun continued to rise.

Even from a half-mile distance, the boy and Hayyel could hear the horses.

"They know," Hayyel said.

"They know we're here?" the boy asked, puzzled by the remark.

"No. They know death is upon them. Only one herd lives after them."

The boy thought for a moment before questioning Hayyel again. "What's gonna happen to you when all the horses are gone?"

"I will go to the reservation and live among my people. I will grow old and the children will point to me and laugh and say 'there goes the old ugly one.'"

The boy chuckled. "So, you really ain't going to Oregon with the rest of 'em?"

"No. My work will be done. Besides, my role as shaman requires that I always stay on Crow land."

"But this ain't Crow land."

"Yes, it is. All the land from the reservation west to the Bear Tooth Mountains was once the land my people claimed. We were proud warriors and descendants of the 'ancient ones.' But the Cheyenne and the Lakota took the land from us. They pushed us against the Bear Tooth and we fought back. We fought together with the US Calvary and Custer and won our land back. We were the good Indians your history books never teach you about. We were the loyal scouts and friends of the white man. And today we are the good people that He-That-Hears-All smiles upon."

The boy chuckled again. "Yeah, but if you'd been re-settled to Oklahoma, your tribe woulda been filthy rich in oil."

"We are rich. Look around. This Crow land is good land. It is rich to the eye and to the heart."

"And your pa? Is that why he stayed? Cuz he loved the land?"

"No. He stayed because he had a job to do. He was our agent until he died. Then, we buried him as a Crow warrior near my cabin." Hayyel stopped his rant. He cupped his hand against an ear and turned towards the wind. "Listen. The horses no longer cry. They rejoice. They sing. They sing of us coming to take them away. They sing of you."

At first, the boy wanted to scoff at the notion but Hayyel's eyes were sincere and he knew better than to insult his friend. "Okay. What are they singing about?"

"They say the boy will save their kind."

"I can't save them."

"But you will."

"No, I won't. You and me, we'll put down their boss and Judas will lead 'em to the stockyards just like we always do. And, one-by-one, we'll butcher 'em just like we did the others."

Hayyel disagreed. He gazed at the sky and at the sun radiating from behind the treetops. He held his palms to the sun and whispered to the wind with his eyes closed. When he finished conversing with his god, he had tears in his eyes. "He-That-Hears-All loves you. He says that you no longer have to shoot the good horses. He says that if you walk with this herd, they will follow you down His mountain."

The boy shook his head and kicked the dirt. "No way. No way will those wild mustangs follow me into that cesspool. Are you crazy? They'd just as soon stomp my ornery hide as look at me."

"But they will follow you. And you will lead them. He-That-Hears-All says this is the last herd my ancestors will ever need in heaven. After we collect this herd my work will be finished."

"But there's one more herd after this one."

"Yes. But they will remain here on the mountain unharmed."

The boy had heard enough. He hoisted the rifle over a shoulder and took off along the tree line without looking back, ranting the entire way. "I'm gonna go do my job. My work ain't finished," he shouted. "I'm gonna shoot the boss like I'm suppose to. I'm gonna collect my pay and wire it to Polly in Hollywood. That's what I'm gonna do. You call the others on the walkie-talkie and do what you're supposed to do."

37

When the boy reached the bend, alone, he crouched low in wheat grass to avoid being detected by the mustangs. He glassed the herd with the binoculars making mental notes of where three mares guarded their fouls and where four yearlings soaked in the watering hole. Two bachelors parked on the hillside nearby, oblivious to his presence; the two sniffed the air as if searching for a ripe mare. The rest of the herd littered about in small bands, frozen in place, staring at imaginary ghosts. The baying that echoed earlier across the mountaintop had ceased altogether. Now, the horses lurked aimlessly about, lingering in silence.

Despite the placidity, the boy had trouble locating the boss stallion and needed to change his position. He crawled through the grass to where the tree line switched back and down to the water for a better look. Without the boss, there'd be no shot taken. Without the crack from rifle fire, Hayyel would never initiate the call to the cowboys who waited a half-mile away on the other side of the meadow.

After ten minutes, the boy had made no more progress discovering the boss's location and was about to move to higher ground when he sensed being watched. He turned his head. A gray dun stallion stood fifty feet to his right. The horse had been there the entire time studying him.

Laying belly-down and vulnerable to an attack, the boy slipped the rifle off a shoulder, rolled on his side, and pointed the barrel at the stallion's chest while discretely disengaging the safety. Through it all, the horse stood motionless with its ears perked forward listening to the boy's slightest sounds. Even as the boy eyed it through the rifle sight, the dun seemed unfazed by the intruder's presence. By the time the boy wrapped a finger around the trigger, the horse had resumed chewing on the grass hanging out of its mouth, oblivious to its impending death. Meanwhile, its tail swatted sporadically at flies.

The situation put the boy in a baffling predicament. With the horse showing no aggression whatsoever (its hind leg kicked back bent and relaxed), what should he do? *Shoot or befriend it?* Wild horses charge when threatened, yet this horse, the presumed aggressive boss stallion, seemed to accept him. Oddly, its eyes showed more curiosity than fear.

Based on this unusual behavior and on what Hayyel professed earlier, the boy decided to speak to the dun in the same calm manner he did with the colt at the arena in Sheridan. He lowered the rifle. "You don't want to latch onto me, fella. I'm bad news for the bunch of you."

Whether the horse understood the boy's words or the soothing tone of the boy's voice lulled it into complacency didn't seem to matter. Either way, the horse never considered the boy a threat. In fact, as soon as the boy finished speaking, the horse moved straight toward the two-legged creature and stood directly in front, sniffing the creature's jeans; the pockets reeked of strawberry rock candy and overpowered the horse's craving for sweets.

The boy rose slowly to his knees and then to his feet, and took the candy out of wrappers and fed the horse, but instinct told him not to press his luck, so he stepped backward in the direction where the cowboys were presumed to be waiting. Once at a safe distance, he twirled around, hitched the rifle over a shoulder, and fast-walked a beeline getaway expecting to get trampled or blindsided. When he glanced back at the dun, it had fallen in line thirty feet behind while the herd had fallen in behind their leader. The boy looked down the tree line toward the cabin. Hayyel was walking in parallel two hundred yards away, lugging the walkie-talkie and waving to him. The boy guessed Hayyel had not radioed the crew.

After an hour, the boy reached the western edge of the great meadow. From that vista, he could make out Black Mesa towering twelve miles away. The sight stirred panic in the boy, and he spun around and raised the flat of his hand in a traditional 'stop' manner. The horses responded by halting in unison. He looked to his left. The cowboys strung out on horseback with the packhorses and Judas weaving through tall firs on the far ridge. They had been following him and the herd all along but from a discrete distance. To his right, Hayyel lumbered head down tackling high grass, trying to maintain a two hundred yard cushion. It was during this interlude that the boy attempted to gather his thoughts on the extraordinary behavior exhibited by the horses. *Just why did they continue to follow him*? He wondered, perplexed by the situation.

The gray dun suddenly let loose with a drawn-out snort as if abdicating the herd leadership. With that the boy felt a compelling need to say something, anything, to the dun and the rest of the horses to get them to back off. The fact is he felt horrible about what was transpiring. "Looky, here, all of you. I don't understand what's going on but if you keep on following me, you're gonna die. I'm heading down there," he said, pointing to the mesa, "where the devil lives. I'd stay the hell away if I was you. Yonder is a bad place. A really bad place." Yet, in spite of the plea, the dun simply blinked its eyes and swatted at flies as it had done before, unconcerned by the warning. Likewise, the other horses seemed unmoved by the speech. "I'm dead serious," the boy pressed. "You best hightail it outta here or a few weeks from now some dog in New York City is gonna have you all over for supper. Sabe?"

Oddly enough, the dun did understand, as did the others. What is more, the mustangs continued to follow the boy even after he told them to go home, even after he resumed walking down the hill toward Potrero Gap.

XXXVIII

Once upon a time I thought about joining the church. Just once. When I was thirteen. It was the church where my Ma and my Pa got married. I remember what got it all going. One evening after supper Henry says to me, "Hey, Squirt, you're supposed to get confirmed when you're in the eighth grade. You ready to join up or you gonna give me another ration of crap about there being no such things as God and heaven?"

Now those words didn't sit well with me. Ticked me off they did. While it was true that I did have my doubts about the Man Upstairs and the afterlife. . . don't we all? I mean who the heck was Henry to question my beliefs or lack of beliefs? And by that age I was getting awful tired of being called 'Squirt.' To me Henry was just being a bully and I the kid brother he could pick on. Then again at age thirteen Henry probably coulda said 'the sky is blue' and that woulda ticked me off too. Anyways. I turned around and smart-mouthed back to him the way I always did. "Oh, yeah, big man? You think you know everything. Prove there's a heaven and I'll get baptized tomorrow." I said.

Well now. Henry grabs me by the neck and yanks me outside. I remember a full moon peeking over the horizon and the stars as clear as I'd ever seen 'em. And Henry points to four bright ones and says, "See those, Squirt?" To which I said, "Yup. Four bright stars lined up in a straight line. So what?" And he says, "You are a numbskull, ain't you? Those aren't stars. Those are planets. Tonight they're perfectly aligned. Won't happen again for seventy-four years."

"Big deal," I said. "I'll be dead and buried in seventy-four years. I don't give a shit." That just made Henry even madder. He slaps me on the side of the head and says, "You don't get it. Do you? This earth of ours is on the same gravitational plane as those four. Look at 'em again."

This time I looked long and hard and after a minute or so it dawned on me that with the earth lined up with those planets we were tilted away from the sun just like I'd learned in school. Without the earth tilting like it did we'd have no seasons. There'd be no winter. No spring. And so forth. Henry must of seen that spark in my eyes cuz he says to me, "Now, do you really think all this happened by accident? You don't think something wonderful come along and set all this in motion for the likes of you and me?"

"You got me, Henry," I said. "It's all too much for this little pea brain of mine to figure out. Let's just get me baptized and be done with it. That way if there's really a heaven and God, I'll be safe at home plate. If not, no harm done."

Now at the time Henry was dating a local girl named Beverly Harris. She was one of those up-tight religious sorts who also dabbled in astrology and the occult. Guess Beverly was covering all the bases too. Well now. Beverly somehow got Henry interested in that bunch of malarkey and he suddenly says to me all serious-like. "We're entering a dark phase," he says. "Dark phase?" I asked. "What in the devil you talking about?" And he says back, "After this alignment, the earth is gonna be hurting for ten years. Mankind is gonna go to hell and back. Things gonna get better around the Age of Aquarius but then bad again around two thousand nine."

On that note I laughed and laughed. I told Henry he and his girlfriend were fulla beans. But the truth of the matter is Henry was right. That year Hitler cranked up the Nazi war machine. World War Two ended ten years later. All them hippies and free-love kind reached a peak just when Henry said they would. And this old world of ours took a turn for the worst right after the second George Bush got ready to leave office. Kinda scary my brother being right so much. Looking back in the rearview mirror Henry doesn't seem so dumb now.

Anyways. Henry being older and wiser decided to follow through with my impulse on getting baptized and arranged to have me dunked at the church the next morning that being on a Sunday at the eight o'clock service. When the time come up to commit oneself to God and Jesus and Whatnot I stood up and the preacher called me down to the front and escorted me behind the altar where a bathtub trough sunk into the floor. Now the preacher he pulls back the tarp covering up that baptismal tub and low-and-behold the thing is empty. The trough had sprung a leak and all the holy water had seeped out. And the preacher he looked at me all mortified and says, "This has never happened before. It's not a good sign. Is it, son?" To which I replied, "Things like this don't happen by accident. Something must of set it all in motion. I don't think I'm supposed to go through with getting baptized."

And I didn't. Years later I often wonder if it was just fool's bad luck that caused that holy water to leak out or if the Man Upstairs just didn't want my ornery hide mucking up his church. I know that sounds blasphemous but when you're bound for hell it doesn't make any difference one way or another. I just knew I wasn't ready to accept the notions of organized religion and the idea of a hereafter.

39

"Son, you have a rare gift."

"A *gift*, Captain?"

"The way you led the horses down the gap by yourself—it was magical. Neither Lieutenant Mullin nor I have ever seen anything like what you did. Did you know you had that ability? To lead horses. Just by talking sweet to them?"

"No, sir. Not until this morning. But I don't think it's gonna happen again."

"And why is that?"

"Because of something Hayyel told me."

"And what did the half-breed say?"

"He said that herd wanted to die. They were giving up. Sacrificing themselves. This last bunch, on the other hand, they don't wantta give up. They wantta live."

"And do you believe the half-breed's nonsense?"

"Not sure. Just know this last bunch won't go down without a fight."

"Then a fight it is we will give them. We know how to put up a good fight and win battles. Don't we Lieutenant Mullin?"

The boy glanced over at the Lieutenant who stood at attention in the hallway half-emerged in the study. Over the course of weeks, the boy had grown to dislike the man. The Lieutenant had been standoffish and arrogant since the day the Beechcraft landed at the entrance road. Worse, the man expressed contempt for Hayyel and the others. That alone set him apart from the boy. Even now, he wore a brutish fake smile attempting to befriend the boy and flatter the Captain.

"Yes, sir. We sure do."

When the boy turned back around Captain Belial had already stood up and was limping to the liquor cabinet for three glasses and a favorite bottle of brandy. He brought the glasses back, filled, shuffled around the desk, and stood by its corner, immersed in the shadowy light cast by the shrouded lamp.

"Come. Have a toast with me, son. You, too, Lieutenant."

The boy rose and twirl-tossed his hat back to the couch. The Lieutenant joined him by the desk and the three raised their glasses together until they clunked.

"Here's to the victory over the feral beasts of Pryor Mountain. One more herd and they will be gone forever."

"Here-here," the Lieutenant mused.

"Cheers," the boy said.

"And to our new expeditionary team," the Captain added.

The boy drew a puzzled look. "What new team?"

"Why, you and the Lieutenant." The Captain paused. The confusion showed in the boy's eyes causing the boy to hesitate before drinking the brandy. "I thought you knew, son. The half-breed has returned to the reservation. He left me a note stating his work here was complete. So, now it is you and the Lieutenant on this final roundup of ours."

A look of disgust swept over the boy's face. He eyed the Lieutenant and then drowned the brandy. "I've got to go," he blurted.

"Where to, son?"

"We've got a hundred forty mustangs down in the pens to dress out. Sully and Bob shouldn't have to do it alone."

The boy snagged his hat and darted down the hallway, past the newspaper headlines on the wall and to the front door without looking back.

40

Miss Edna's patrons swarmed the first floor parlor the minute the place opened its doors. Word got out how after twenty years at Pryor Mountain the cowboys were moving to Oregon. One of the locals organized the surprise party—an odd combination cowboy and mustang bon voyage celebration. Between the highly publicized word-of-mouth invites and the drinks-are-on-the-house circulars, the house packed solid. Besides the three cowboys and Miss Edna's girls (minus Polly) and Beulah and Big Mike and Miss Edna, the gathering also included the mayor and his councilmen, the parish priest, the entire Federal Grazing Service managerial staff, and a handful of Mormons from Sheridan. Those conspicuously absent included the Sheriff and his deputies and one Bert Modene, the town drunk, who, rumor had it, was spending the night in the town hoosegow.

Almost from the get-go, some of the more eloquently inebriated benefactors began praising the PMRC crew as twentieth century heroes. Others hailed the three cowboys as Montana's answer to the brave new world. Some gave bombastic speeches about the old west dying and the new west belonging to cattlemen and purveyors of the electronic age. But the locals who truly knew their whorehouse comrades fretted how their friends' presence would be sorely missed. Miss Edna's girls would especially miss their fun-loving patrons. Befitting the evening's mood, the girls bared all except black sashes draped across their more intimate body parts. Finally, after all the initial commotion settled, everyone in the house began chanting for a speech from the cowboys. It didn't take much coaxing to get Sully to exercise his oratory skills.

"Thank you all for this, here, send-off. Bob and me and the kid can think a just one thing that woulda this night more complete."

"Free poontang," Bob hollered out. "*EeeHaa.*"

Everyone laughed at the notion but Big Mike. He began moving about the parlor with his hat held out collecting loose change to honor Bob's wish, using a velvet hammer shakedown. Few denied Big Mike loose change.

"Indeed. Free poontang would sure be nice and all that," Sully continued, "but what woulda been nicer was if our friend, Hayyel Gabriel coulda been here tonight with us. He returned yesterday to the reservation. We'll miss him."

Someone yelled out, "Who the hell is Hayyel Gabriel?"

"You know who he is," Sully fired back. He stopped long enough to spit chaw and wipe off his mouth. "*The Chief.*"

"Oh. The Chief." The man acknowledged in a matter-of-fact manner.

Everyone nodded his or her head. Everyone knew 'The Chief.'

"But I just wantta say we'll miss you all, too. Especially you, Edna. You are one special whore if there ever was one."

Edna was the last lady of the evening still wearing clothes. She blushed and then sauntered to where Sully stood, favoring her good leg, and took him by the hand. "Why, Sully. You do know how to flatter a girl," she said. "Tonight you can take me for free."

Everyone cheered on that note. Bob patted his friend on the shoulder and the boy almost dropped his cigarette from laughter. The woman rubbing up against the boy still hadn't managed to get the boy's attention and continued pressuring him on her earlier proposal.

"Like I said, Sugar, for five dollars I can help you forget all about Polly." The woman had yet to get a straight answer from the boy who had been distracted by the festivities and the free drinks, and had done his level best to ignore her. Frustrated, the woman repositioned herself in front of the boy, blocking his view and forcing him to look her in the eyes. That's when she noticed his eyes. "Say, Sugar, did anyone ever tell you you've got gorgeous peepers? How about me lowering the price to two-fifty just because of those eyes of yours?"

"That's awful kind of you Ma'am, but I think I'll stick with Polly, if that's alright?"

"Why, sure it's alright, Sugar. But don't forget, Polly is the one who scrammed out of here a week ago. And she hasn't called or sent you a telegram, yet. Has she?"

"No. She hasn't. She's probably going through all kinds of screen tests right now and those sorts of things take time. Hollywood's a busy place, don't you know."

"I'm sure it is. But—" The woman stopped mid-sentence as the thought struck. "Say, you're still a virgin, aren't you?"

"Yes, Ma'am, and I'm saving it for Polly."

The woman shook her head in disbelief and kissed the boy on the cheek. "I think that's awfully swell. Why, you giving Polly all that money and taking care of her like you are, every girl here should be so gosh darned lucky. Tell you what you and I can do that Polly shouldn't have one bit of problem with."

"What's that, Ma'am?"

"*Dance.*"

The woman snatched a dime out of Big Mike's hat as he passed by and quick-foot waltzed to the new jukebox to select a tune. She spun back around once the music started blaring, and eyed the boy. Her black sash slid off her breasts to her hips and black panties, and left nothing to the boy's imagination. She untied her hair and shook it loose to her shoulders, and started gyrating and singing with the music.

"*Jeepers creepers, where'd you get those peepers? Jeepers creepers, where'd you get those eyes. . . .*"

As she moved to the boy everyone started clapping in rhythm to the music.

"*. . . Gosh all git-up. How'd you get so lit up? Gosh all git-up. How'd it get that size?*"

She pawed the boy's hand. "Come on, Sugar, let's dance. Let's light up this joint."

The woman mesmerized the boy. As he took a step toward her, a hand squeezed the back of his neck. The hand belonged to Sheriff John Toms.

"Son, I need to see you outside."

41

The boy stepped out on the front porch with the Sheriff. There, a grim looking deputy waited hat in-hand. The youthful deputy grimaced while choking the brim of his Mountie-styled hat. His eyes darted from the boy, then to the Sheriff. "Did you tell him, Sheriff?"

The boy looked at them both. The Sheriff still had a hand on the boy's neck and started to tear up.

"It's Polly, ain't it?" the boy asked.

The Sheriff nodded 'yes.'

"She's dead. Right?"

The Sheriff couldn't speak. The deputy took his cue. "We found her on the roof of the Rialto. She's been up there for a week. Some folks noticed a foul smell and—"

"I want to see her."

"I don't think you want to do that, son," the Sheriff interjected. "She's in a bad way. Between the sun and the flies and the crows—"

"Sir. I've seen more death than you and all your deputies put together. Now, I want to see her."

The Sheriff decided it best not to argue with the boy. The three walked the short distance to the movie house in silence. The boy never asked how she died but had his own idea. They climbed the rear stairway to the rooftop and were greeted by two deputies taking photographs. The roof lit bright from the neon spire. The girl's body slumped naked in a corner and lay visible in flashes of red and green and yellow. Her dress still heaped in a pile ten feet away. The crows and flies had gotten to her eyes, and her skin had bleached and shrunk from the sun. Maggots oozed from her open and festered mouth. A stench filled the air and the two deputies wore bandanas around their noses to screen the smell. In spite of the conditions, the boy walked straight to within a foot of Polly's body and stared down at her.

"We recovered all that money you gave her, son," the Sheriff said. "Well, most of it. What she didn't use to shoot up with."

The boy looked at her hand frozen on the syringe and the hypodermic needle still inserted in the arm.

"Looks like she got a bad batch of the stuff. I'm sorry, son. Really sorry."

The boy said nothing. He took a step back and looked up at the night sky. He spotted Mars to the east and Venus dancing low on the horizon. He gazed at Orion and the Big Dipper and the myriad of stars glimmering overhead. Everything in the universe appeared lined up the way it was supposed to, except for Polly. He looked at her again, this time sadly. "Ain't she grand," he said.

"What's that, son?"

The boy turned to the Sheriff and spoke louder. "I said, *ain't she grand*."

42

They spotted the herd from the Beechcraft's windows and circled for ten minutes while taking a count. As fortune would have it, the mustangs had migrated to the same watering hole as the herd removed a week before. This bunch, too, would be an easy capture. Once a count had been taken, T.F. managed to land the craft below Penn's cabin, this in spite of a thunderstorm igniting in the early morning sky. T.F. wished the two cowboys best of fortune on their final roundup as he was returning the plane to Denver for maintenance. They all shook hands. The boy and the Lieutenant watched as the Beechcraft soared out of the canyon and took its bearing to the southeast.

Three days had passed since they discovered Polly's body. During that time, the boy located where an aunt in Spokane was raising Polly's baby, wired the woman the last of his money, and mailed off Polly's personal belongings. The day before, they held a small funeral for the girl in Laurel. The boy paid for the casket and flowers and the gravestone marker as well as the parish priest, though he wasn't sure if Polly practiced Catholicism. He figured having the priest say a few words couldn't hurt. Polly laid to rest in a cemetery plot next to the mayor's family. Martha and John Toms attended the service as did Sully and Bob and Miss Edna and the girls. No one else came or dared to attend the funeral of a common whore. In fact, most townsfolk seemed incensed over the entire situation. For days, the town stewed in the details of the girl's grisly death. Rumors began circulating how Miss Edna's boarding house would get shut down by the end of the week. It was bad enough Laurel hosted a brothel, but the thought that the quaint community on the banks of the Yellowstone River also housed drug addicts proved too much for everyone, even for those still imbued with old-style Wild West morals.

In a sense, Polly had been better taken care of in death than in life. So, after everyone left the cemetery and paid his or her last respects to the girl, Billy stayed, hat in-hand, and touched the casket one last time before having it lowered into the ground. "I know you wanted to be a star, Polly," he whispered, "but to me you always were and always will be. And I will always love you."

Since then, the boy had said little else to anyone. To say he felt depressed would be an understatement. In his brief existence, he had experienced the tragic loss of the three people he loved the most. Now, with Polly gone, the Pryor job about to go away, and being flat broke, his future appeared bleak. And there was one gnawing aspect about this final roundup driving him to an even lower depth—the mustangs, too, would be gone forever. Through all of the killing and butchering, he had discovered newfound respect for the horses. They had become symbolic of his life and the people he lost. Still, he always thought the mustangs would be around on Pryor Mountain. Now they were about to become extinct and a waning memory in a cavalcade of waning memories.

Even as the boy and Lieutenant Mullin disembarked the plane and walked to the ridge where Penn's cabin stood, few words passed between them. The Lieutenant never mentioned the girl's death or showed any concern over the boy's anguish. The man's attention, understandably, focused on the capture of the herd. After all, this day was the culmination of twenty years of hard work. It should have been no surprise when the Lieutenant offered to lug the weighty walkie-talkie backpack and perform the lowly grunt logistics. Anything that helped this last mission succeed played into the greater scheme of 'full and final victory' over the horses. Besides, the boy's job included both tracking and shooting the boss stallion; the boy couldn't be expected to do everything.

When the boy did speak, he explained to the Lieutenant that he was already familiar with the terrain and, therefore, knew the best location for scouting the herd. The Lieutenant could remain at the cabin with the walkie-talkie, out of the rain while listening for rifle fire or tag along. The Lieutenant chose to tag along.

With the boy in the lead, they hiked following the tree line bordering the expansive eastern meadow. After they rounded the bend in the trees, the boy knelt hidden behind a bush while glassing the watering hole and the surrounding hillside where the Spanish mustangs clustered in family bands. Nothing obvious or unusual stood out. He did locate the white colt he had won in Sheridan standing with the rear vanguard and contentedly munching grass with other young bachelors. The colt had already assimilated into the herd and seemed at ease waiting for its chance to become a boss. The boy watched as the lead mares sauntered through the meadow and nudged young foals toward the water. But, like the week before, the herd's boss stallion was nowhere to be found. For an hour, the boy moved in and out of strategic vantages, including the woods bordering the meadow, in an attempt to locate the leader. Finally, he gave up. "You need to have Sully and Bob release Judas. Maybe Judas can draw him out," he conceded.

The Lieutenant radioed in the request and within ten minutes Judas came galloping full throttle to the waterhole with his tail tall and erect, showing off every bit of his black bravado. By now, the rain had turned into a steady drizzle and thunder began rumbling across the mountaintop. Lightning flashed behind Judas and accentuated his apparition out of the west from beyond the crest of the hill. The two cowboys watched as the black horse barreled into the middle of the herd and bucked yearlings aside, all this as a heavy downpour erupted. The cold rain stirred Judas with even more anger and he shook his head as if he had gone mad, but not before butting the lead mare to the ground. He circled around and returned near the crest of the meadow to savor the commotion he caused, only to burst through the herd once again, this time sparing and kicking in an attempt to draw out the boss. When no boss emerged, he whickered for the entire lot to follow or face his fury. Suddenly, a challenger emerged from the shadows of the trees, charging to the herd's rescue.

"*Shit*. It's Old White," the Lieutenant muttered. "I thought you killed him?"

The boy had trouble believing his eyes and scoped the animal with the binoculars for a better sighting. Indeed, the white horse had somehow survived the gunshot. Blood still oozed from the shoulder wound where the slug fragmented after striking bone. Judging by the shoveled gait, the boy knew the horse moved in great pain. "I shot him just like we talked about but we never could find his remains. He got washed down—"

"I don't give a damn what happened. Just shoot him again before he kills Judas."

By now, the two horses had engaged in battle and twirled in a tight circle, biting and jabbing each other. The boy slid the rifle off his shoulder, disengaged the safety, and fumbled with the aperture. Prepping for the shot through the rain took valuable seconds; seconds he didn't have. From less than two hundred yards the kill would be doable. Still, with the horses spinning and kicking, any shot taken might hit the wrong horse. Meanwhile, Sully and Bob had already galloped over the crest of the meadow and were within the same distance as the boy to where the horses skirmished. The boy knew if he didn't take the shot, Bob would take one on the run.

"Damn it all, kid, shoot that white horse," the Lieutenant screamed again, trying to be heard above the rain.

It was then that the white horse slipped and fell on his back. Judas came down hard stomping the boss stallion's chest. Judas reared a second time but the boy let loose with a round to its head. The black horse stumbled sideways and splashed to the ground. The white horse rolled to his feet, shook himself dry, and then bayed to the herd. Moments later, the mustangs began stampeding toward the woods and out of harms way as the white horse pushed them onward from behind.

Furious, the Lieutenant let loose with a flurry of blows to the boy's face, breaking the boy's nose with the first punch. The boy fell to the ground and reached for his Winchester but the Lieutenant kicked the rifle out of the way and then tossed it into the woods. With a boot planted on the boy's chest, he threatened to do more harm. "You little son-of-a-bitch. You know what you just did? You just let this last herd escape. And you killed Captain Belial's favorite horse. It'll take the Captain years to train another one. You messed this up good for everyone."

Blood ran down the boy's face. He looked up and smiled defiantly. "Good. I shoulda killed that devil horse first time I seen it."

With that, the Lieutenant squared back and walloped the boy where he lay, knocking the boy into unconsciousness.

43

"How many fingers am I holding up, kid?"

The boy recognized Sully's voice but his head hurt so much all he could do was moan. He tried to open his eyes but one swelled shut and the other caked in blood and would barely prop halfway. When he went to wipe the dried blood away, he discovered his hands tied behind his back; he had been hogtied upright on a horse and facing backwards. He peered skyward with the good eye and could tell it was after sunset. The western horizon hung dark blue with shades of red. That meant he had been out cold for at least twelve hours. It explained why his lips and tongue parched. Before he could utter the word 'water,' his head began throbbing. Everything spun and for a few seconds he thought he might pass out but Sully threw cold water on his face and re-ignited consciousness. Now dripping wet, he looked around to gain his bearings and noticed that he and the horse sat under the Π-shaped front entrance to the PMRC. The horse faced the camp. He faced west. "Where am I? How'd I get here?" he asked, mumbling.

"Easy there, kid. One question at a time. First, you're back at Potrero Gap and the camp. Second, Bob and I hitched you to that horse seeing as how you were bleedin' all over the place and passed out. Why, if we hadn't a pulled Lieutenant Mullin off you when we did, you'd be dead right now. You were takin' a terrible beatin'. And if it hasn't dawned on you yet, you got a few broken ribs, a busted jaw and nose, and you're minus some upper teeth."

"That's right, kid. You and me now got something in common," Bob stated a little too gleefully. "We're both missin' our uppers."

The boy's tongue felt the holes left in the gums of his mouth and he wanted to cry out but when he tried to take a deep breath the pain was excruciating and he froze. "Untie me. *Now*," he muttered.

Sully reached around the horse and slid the ropes off the boy's shoulder and from around the saddle and saddle horn that had kept him upright.

"And untie my hands," the boy added.

"Sorry, kid. No can do. Captain's orders."

"What do you mean?"

"I mean you upset the Captain. I told you. . . hell, we all told you not to get crossways with him. He's plenty mad at you."

"Damn it, Sully. Untie me."

"Whoa, kid," Bob butted in. "There'll be plenty a time for cursin' later. Right now we're just doin' what we're told to do."

"And looky over yonder," Sully interjected. "Here comes the Captain as we speak. I've never seen him outside the big house. You sure riled him good, kid. That's all I can say."

The boy craned his neck around and watched the Captain limp down the camp road with Lieutenant Mullin propping him up by the shoulder. The boy also noticed the music blaring from the big house. Playing was the Boston Symphony version of Mahler's *The Adagietto*. He knew the music was a bad sign.

The Captain appeared pale and exhausted. He wore an old picador's sombrero to keep what little light remained from striking his face. Neither man would make eye contact with the boy until they maneuvered around the horse. Then, the Captain deliberated while the Lieutenant stepped back wearing a death mask smirk. "Well, son, you have greatly disappointed me. I thought you'd be the one to help end this madness on Pryor Mountain. Instead, I shall be departing for Oregon in a few days without having fully completed my mission."

The words angered the boy. "You and your mission can go to hell."

"Unfortunately, son, you will be going to hell long before me."

"What do you mean?"

"I mean everything I warned you about is coming to fruition. You broke our pact. You stole the life of my prized stallion, which, in itself, is tantamount to horse thievery. And you snatched complete and unconditional victory from my grasp. You must now suffer the consequences. Woe be unto you."

"Oh, yeah? And just who are you to make threats?"

"Son, I don't make threats. I make promises. I can do so because I am your master. I am your alpha and your omega. You belonged to me the day you sealed our pact with a handshake."

"So, what do you want us to do with the kid?" Sully asked.

"Hang him," the Captain answered without remorse.

"But, sir, we don't hang people over horses no more. You're kidding, right?"

"When have I ever kidded you and Bob, Sully. Just do my bidding." The Captain did an about face and limped unescorted back up the road toward the big house. He never looked back.

"You heard the Captain, you two," Lieutenant Mullin spouted. "Get to it."

Bob threw a rope over the entrance cross support and began fashioning a noose. Sully kept yakking nervously. "This is all a joke, ain't it? You all are just scarin' the kid to teach him a lesson. Right? You don't really intend to hang him. Do ya? Look, Lieutenant, you've already beaten the boy to a bloody pulp. Ain't that lesson enough? Come on, now. Can't we talk about this?" No one paid any attention to Sully. He turned to Bob for an appeal. "Bob, you don't wantta do this. Not to the kid. Leave him be. He's just a baby. We don't hang babies."

Bob snarled. "The hell we don't. How about the bullet you put in the back of young Dante Alegre's head?"

"That was different. He was gonna tell the Sheriff about what we did down in Texas. Squeal he was. The kid, here, would take what he knows to the grave before he'd turn on us. He's a cut above."

"Makes no difference, Sully. We do what we're told to do. Remember the pact."

"So the Captain says hang the kid and you're just gonna hang the kid. Is that it? You a company man through and through. Is that it?"

"Indeed, I am, Sully. So are you. Now outta my way." Bob finished the noose and shoved Sully aside. He climbed up the horse and faced the boy, looping the rope around the boy's neck and drawing the slack out to stretch it tight. The boy winced in pain unable to breathe. Bob leaped off. "Ready," he said to the Lieutenant.

The Lieutenant tied down the other end of the rope, then pulled out his sidearm and announced he would fire it to spook the horse.

Sully moved in front of the horse and held it secure by the reins. "What are you afraid of, Bob?"

"Tell you what I'm afraid of, Sully. I'm afraid of goin' to hell."

"Didn't think you believed in hell, Bob."

"I lied."

"Fine. So, you lied and now you're afraid of goin' there. Shoot. Look around you. Look at what you've done with your life. You're goin' one way or another, anyways. You think the Captain isn't takin' you there on his coattails? Way I look at it, you got one chance to set it all right. And this is it. Now do the right thing. Spare this boy."

Bob glared at Sully but, realizing his partner had a point, decided to glance at the boy one last time. And as he watched the boy squirm, shame overcame him. He loved the boy. *What was he doing?* With little forethought, he dug in his shirt pocket, fished out the Indian head penny and flipped it in the air to Sully. "Here," he said. "You keep it. Don't let 'em ever say old Bob broke all the Commandments, leastways turned his back on his friends." He spun around and took a step toward the Lieutenant who still brandished the revolver.

The Lieutenant stepped back cocking the gun as he moved. "Take another step and I'll put a bullet in Sully's head. Got it?"

Sully spoke up. "Let him do it, Compadre. I'm ready for the hereafter. . . *God bless Texas.*"

Bob leaped for the gun but came up short, slipped and fell. The Lieutenant fired and Sully's head jerked back. Brain matter sprayed the horse. The horse spooked and sprung forward leaping over Sully's body, leaving the boy suspended in the air by the rope. Bob got off the ground and ran to the boy. He tried lifting the boy up by the legs but struggled getting nowhere. "Stand on my shoulders, kid. Stand on my shoulders," he kept pleading, but the rope was too tight and the boy's legs jerked about.

The Lieutenant found the predicament amusing and began laughing. "Know what, Bob?" he asked, more as a statement. "I never liked dumb-ass cowboys like you—and I never liked Texans, neither." He took measured aim and shot Bob twice in the back. Bob fell dead next to his friend.

By now, the boy had worked his hands free and swung them up to grasp the rope and support the full weight of his body. With his strength sapped, he knew holding on would be futile. The Lieutenant walked in front to study the boy's bloated face. "Looks like you'll be joining your friends shortly, *Compadre. . . .*"

44

For over a week Hayyel Gabriel had camped alone atop Bopwadesh Hill awaiting a sign. Days earlier, while he slept at the camp bunkhouse, a vision came to him for a second time. He knew better than to ignore visions. He-That-Hears-All never speaks to men in dreams more than twice. In the vision the boy and the white horse named Remliel had become united, and it was glorious. The boy had become a human being and Remliel had become the boy's spirit horse. The two galloped as one over grassy plains and none of the Crow warriors of old could catch them as they raced. There were also a white man, a white woman, a yellow dog, and the girl, and they cheered for the boy-horse using white man's words. And He-That-Hears-All smiled upon them all. But just when the boy-horse got ready to cross the finish line, the boy turned around and rode the horse backwards. Doing so, the boy did not see the giant mountain lion that came and devoured them both. That's when He-That-Hears-All spoke: you must protect my child from the evil one. Hayyel did not need to be told three times.

So, with his work completed at the PMRC and his ancestors riding an abundance of spirit horses in heaven, Hayyel ascended the hill and waited for his sign. He watched from the hilltop when the flatbed Ford went to town, and he wondered why the cowboys stayed three nights in Laurel. And he watched when the Beechcraft took off for the last roundup but never came back. Then, when the cowboys returned on horseback from the mountain with no mustangs and the boy riding his horse backwards, he knew this was the sign he had been waiting for, and he collected his things and began his descent back through the gap.

45

". . . and you and me and the Captain could have made a lot of money in Oregon. That ability of yours to talk to mustangs is uncanny. But, it looks like we'll have to find some new recruits and a new Judas horse. Sorry about your friends. And I'm sorry the half-breed isn't here to see all of this. He would have—"

"*He would have what?*" Hayyel stepped forward out of the dusk wielding his hunting knife.

"Well, Chief, I'm glad you could make it to our little Montana necktie party. Now you get to witness firsthand what happens to white men who break their pact with—"

"The evil one."

"I was going to say, 'Captain Belial.' But call him what you like."

"Cut the boy down."

"Nope. Not going to happen. I give the boy about another thirty seconds before he gives up. And with me holding this gun, I can assure you we'll get to see if he lasts that—"

Hayyel flung the knife hoping to catch the Lieutenant off guard but the knife missed the intended target, the Lieutenant's heart. It glanced off the man's forehead with the weighty handle-end knocking him unconscious. As the Lieutenant fell, he managed to squeeze off one shot striking the Crow scout in the abdomen. Hayyel keeled over limping to where the Lieutenant lay moaning. He kicked the revolver into the bushes and retrieved his knife, and handed it to the boy who cut himself down. Then, he collapsed next to his cowboy friends and the boy who sprawled facedown on the dirt road.

46

By the time dawn arrived, the boy had recovered enough of his faculties to sit up and take note of his surroundings. Sully and Bob lay together in a pool of blood. Hayyel had crawled to one of the entrance timber supports and was using it to prop up his back. Hayyel two-finger waved to the boy signaling he was still alive, but barely. "A sad lot we are," he muttered. "Sully and Bob, they are dead. You and me, we are halfway there."

The boy struggled to his feet and staggered to where Hayyel sat in the dirt. He fell to his knees and opened Hayyel's shirt to check the wound. Hayyel had managed to stuff cloth in the entry hole and stop the external bleeding but the hole centered over the liver and the boy knew the inevitable outcome.

"You've seen this before. Yes?"

"Yes," said the boy.

"It is bad?"

"Yes. There's nothing that can be done."

"How much time do I have?"

"A few hours. Half a day."

At first Hayyel said nothing. He winced at the prospect of remaining alive that long with the excruciating pain. "I slept for a few hours," he said. "When I awoke the Lieutenant, he had gone. I think he took the Ford and left."

"Why do you think that?"

"Because he ran over my foot on the way out and nearly over you."

The boy glanced down at Hayyel's right foot. It bent ninety degrees backward.

"I guess he did," was all the boy could say.

"I think the Captain is still in the big house."

The boy strained his eyes to see the front porch light. The sun still hid below the mountain. The morning shadows made the porch light appear like a beacon. The music from the record player still blared. The record was stuck on the same four notes and playing over-and-over. "Does he have a gun?" the boy asked.

"Maybe."

The boy turned around and looked towards the bush. "Looks like the Lieutenant found his."

"Yes."

The boy thought for a few seconds. His entire body hurt and he wanted to lie back down and sleep but he knew he couldn't. "Why didn't he finish us off when he had a second chance?"

"I do not know."

That said, the boy could no longer ignore his own pain. He touched his swollen nose. The bone twisted at an angle and throbbed to the point where he felt death itself might be preferable.

"I can fix your nose."

The boy gave a half-smile. "Touch it, and I'll fix yours."

Hayyel tried to smile, too, but hurt too much. "You know," he said, "we do have a gun."

The boy looked at him and nodded his head. "So, you think the bell gun is still at the kill chute? In the cabinet?"

"Should be. There is a box full of twenty-two cartridges."

The boy stood and staggered toward the stockade in the direction of the kill chute. "I'll only need one," he said over his shoulder.

47

After he kicked open the front door, the voice inside beckoned him back to the study. The voice was almost non-discernable above the blare of the music. The boy walked over to the Victrola and threw it hard against the wall. The antique crashed into pieces. He spun around and followed the light down the newspaper-plastered hallway and to the desk where Captain Belial waited.

"Come in, son. I've been expecting you."

"Where's the Lieutenant?" the boy demanded.

"He drove to town. He had to report the robbery and killings. I expect him and the authorities back here soon. Very soon."

The boy cocked his head. The Captain's answer made little sense. "*Robbery*? What robbery?"

"Why the money you and the half-breed stole from me. As you can plainly see, my safe has been broken into and all my money is missing. Sully and Bob tried to stop you but you shot them down in cold blood. The Indian even tried to knife the Lieutenant but my rescuer escaped with a nasty bump on his head attempting to defend me."

"You don't expect anyone to believe that crock of shit do you?"

"Oh, they will, son. I have powerful interests with the state. And the railroad, I might add. They will believe everything I tell them. And they will hunt you down and, no doubt, shoot you on the run. Your only corroborating witness will be dead shortly of the wound inflicted upon him when he attempted to take Lieutenant Mullin's life. There will be no one left to support your version of what took place. No one left to believe you. And no one to come to your rescue."

The boy thought things through for a few seconds. "And you? How do you figure in all this?"

"Me? I will be the main reason they come after you."

"And why's that?"

"Because you will kill me just like you did the others."

The boy nodded his head. He placed the bell gun on the desk but kept a secure grip on its trigger. "I'm thinking on it."

"What's there to think on, son? An opportunity to kill the likes of me comes along but once. Take the shot while there's still time."

The boy shrugged his shoulders. "What's the point? You're not worth a bullet."

"The point, son, is all of this is part of a plan. A grand plan that you are just a pawn within. In the end, you will do me in. You will add the finishing touch to my hallway of headlines. In a few days the news in Billings will flash, '*COWBOY KILLS CREW AT POTRERO GAP.*' And you and I will live together in infamy in newsprint."

"You'd like that wouldn't you?"

"Absolutely." The Captain seized the boy's hand, the one taunting the bell gun's trigger, and placed the gun's cone muzzle tight against his own forehead, above and between his eyes. "The dimple on my forehead is the target, son. Aim straight and true to the dimple and our worlds will unite forever. Pull the trigger and avenge the horses and the demise of your comrades and the many ills in your short life like the loss of the whore. Send me back to the bosom of hell where I belong." He leaned into the gun and spread his arms wide to embrace death.

"So, you wantta go to hell? Is that it? I'll send you to hell you crazy son-of-a-bitch." The boy pulled the trigger. The Captain's head whiplashed and then crashed straight down on the desk. Blood oozed onto the desktop. The boy tossed the gun on the floor and walked away without looking back.

48

The boy returned to Hayyel with a saddled a horse. He had packed provisions for their getaway and their horse now weighed heavy with saddlebags and the prospect of human bondage. He told Hayyel about the exchange of words in the big house and insisted they leave before the authorities arrive. Thus, the two rode tandem up through the gap and when they reached the top of the pass looked back and saw the flatbed Ford and squad cars racing past the timber entrance with sirens blaring. They watched as the deputies charged into the big house and scurried about looking for the killers. Through the binoculars the boy could make out Lieutenant Mullin pointing to them on the hillside. The boy knew it would be just a matter of time, perhaps a few hours, before a posse assembled to hunt them down.

Earlier, as they rode through the gap, Hayyel had said he wanted to spend his final moments on Bopwadesh Hill. So, the boy redirected the horse toward the aspens and the small meadow where the two had conducted the horse spirit ceremonies. When they reached the spot where Hayyel had camped out observing the goings on of the PMRC, the boy helped his friend off the horse and found the old Indian rug and spread it out. He helped Hayyel disrobe and sit on the rug for what would be the last ritual honoring the dead.

"You must go," Hayyel told the boy. "They will be here soon. Go to my cabin and stay there. It is on good Crow land. They are not allowed on the reservation and will not come after you. When the first snow falls, leave and go to Laurel and ride a train and leave Montana for good. Never return. Never."

The boy understood. He handed Hayyel the ceremonial hunting knife and shook his friend's hand and thanked him for saving his life. "Remember," Hayyel said, "He-That-Hears-All loves you and will protect you."

The boy took off riding toward the mountaintop. When he got less than a hundred yards away from the aspens, Hayyel began chanting to the Crow ancestors. Hayyel told them he would be joining them soon and asked them to prepare a light that he could follow to their hunting grounds. He chanted about other things, too. . . about the boy's pure heart, about the bountiful Crow land on earth and about the spirit horse he would soon be riding in heaven.

After Sheriff John Toms and his deputies dismounted, they noticed Hayyel's eyes closed in meditation. Hayyel faced the west sitting on his knees, naked, with a strand of hair clenched in one hand and a knife readied in the other. The four men walked to within a safe distance. The knife served as a warning to keep back. The Sheriff spoke first. "Chief, I don't want any trouble out of you. Now, where's Billy? . . . *Are you even listening to me?*"

Hayyel blinked opened his eyes and struggled to his feet. He kept his arm bent back, brandishing the knife. "You are on sacred land. Leave."

Earlier the deputies had drawn their revolvers but now, out of fear, cocked them ready.

"Look, Chief, I don't understand what exactly is going on here, but I do know Billy and I find it hard to believe he'd kill two men in cold blood. Two men who were his friends. And then try and kill another over money. That's not the Billy I know. I need to find him. Where is he?"

Sweat cascaded off Hayyel's forehead. Delirium had set in hours earlier as he lay dying. Yet, even crazed with fever, he knew the Sheriff's words made no sense. "*Two men?*" he asked. "What about the third one? The evil one?"

The Sheriff drew a puzzled expression.

"Captain Belial," Hayyel pressed, "he is not dead?"

The Sheriff shook his head 'no.' "That bell gun Billy used, a twenty-two, can't shoot through metal. The Captain has a steel plate in his forehead from the war. He's still alive."

Upon hearing the words 'still alive,' Hayyel began laughing hysterically in madness. He yanked out tufts of hair while beseeching the sky for answers. Convinced that more than just an evil spirit had deceived them, he became furious for there was nothing he could do to change the situation except remain silent as to the boy's whereabouts. Out of desperation, he jabbed the knife at the four men and screamed, "You are all ignorant." Then, choosing to face death, he began his lament, shouting at the four while pounding his chest:

> "My name is Hayyel Gabriel and I am a human being. I am the proud shaman son of Runs-With-Deer, daughter of the Crow Nation. I am the proud shaman son of Winston Gabriel, Yankee son of the city of New York and Federal Agent to the Crow people. I bleed Crow and I bleed Yankee. I bow to no man. I bow only to He-That-Hears-All."

He leaped at the deputies and they gunned him down, ending his anguish.

XLIX

In nineteen thirty-seven I got my first taste of living by myself. Of being independent and being a man. So to speak. I was fifteen at the time. I remember it well because in March of that year Henry got an attack of appendicitis and nearly died. His appendix ruptured and his whole body festered up. The hospital held onto him for two months and when he did come back home he had to lay up for two more. So during that four-month stretch I got to run the funeral home by my lonesome. Did everything. Balanced the books. Sold services to the bereaved. Did the embalming and laying out of the departed. Coordinated with the cemetery. Drove the hearse. Worked as janitor. Wore all the hats is what I did. Heck. Someone had to pay for Henry's bills.

And being the man of the hour I didn't have time for school neither. Had to drop out to take care of family matters. That all happened my sophomore year. The next fall when I re-enrolled they put me back with the kids a year younger. Very humiliating. After all I had just run a high-profile funeral home. How could they expect me to hang out with younger kids most of whom couldn't even drive a car? And I guess that's about the same time I got a bad case of the dumb-ass cuz my grades went to hell in a hand basket. Truth is I quit caring about a formal education. You see I'd grown up. Thought of myself as an adult. Didn't have time for childish ways anymore. Either way it's awful hard to go back down a road you already traveled.

So one day in June of that same year a woman came into my office sobbing up a storm. She was with the circus folks that had just arrived in Billings on the train. They were putting on a show at the fairgrounds next to the rail yard. Turns out she was one of the circus acts. Quite the looker she was. Now mind you back in the thirties they had what was called peep shows. You'd pay a dime to look through a tent hole and you'd get to watch a girl naked. Well. Half-naked. But it didn't matter none because women back then were much more modest than nowadays with the mini-skirt and tube-top and whatnot. So half-naked in nineteen thirty-seven was like being fully clothed in two thousand nine. Especially to a fifteen-year-old boy with a perpetual boner. Did I mention she was stacked?

So this good-looking and well-stacked woman comes into the office needing help. She says her manager had just choked to death eating a ham sandwich and needed to be buried proper-like. Needed the full treatment he did. The man's name was Louis Dupree but everyone called him Big Lou. And he owned and managed the OoLaLa Cabaret Girls and had a pot full of money. Cost was no object according to this woman. And we looked at all of our caskets and she rejected 'em one-by-one. Let me tell you something. We had expensive caskets and the woman wanted no part of 'em. Wernt be-fitting her benefactor she said. None of 'em.

Now a few months earlier Henry had ordered us a pipe organ. The type that you pump the baffles up with your feet and the music comes out through pipes in the back. It was a big deal back in the day. If you didn't have one for your parlor you couldn't compete with the other funeral home in town. So Henry orders us one. Cost a lotta money. More money than what we had. Of course he did this without consulting me cuz I was just a fifteen-year-old squirt who didn't know a thing about running a business. Anyways. I walk this woman past our storage room and she looks in and says, "That casket will be perfect," and she points to the huge wooden crate the organ came in. I couldn't believe my ears. I said to her, "Lady, that's not a casket. That's an organ crate." And she says back to me, "Oh, you haven't seen Big Lou. He's nearly five hundred pounds. That's the only thing big enough to fit him in." Turns out Big Lou was also the circus fat man. He got billed as 'The World's Fattest Man.' And he was.

So the woman asks if the crate can be painted gold to give Big Lou's sendoff some class and I said, "Sure. For a price." I figured if Big Lou had money he'd only want top dollar paid for his crate-casket. And I sold her what I coined 'the crasket' for eight hundred dollars. Cash. Heck. Our best floor casket was the 'Prince of Peace' and it only cost five hundred. Next the woman wanted to know about flowers and embalming and everything else. Normally those sorts of expenses would run two or three hundred dollars. I told her not to worry none. A cool four thousand dollars would take care of everything. Crasket and all. The woman didn't bat an eyelash. She dug into her purse and pulled out the money and threw in an extra hundred cuz she said I'd been sweet to her.

Well. I went down to the rail yard and found me eight able bodied men. All hobos. And paid 'em ten dollars each to carry Big Lou the six-block distance to the funeral home. Right down Main Street stopping traffic they went. Let me tell you they earned their pay and then some. Later I discovered Big Lou was too big to fit in our basement morgue so he got put out on the backyard picnic table. I turned on two fans to keep the flies away and embalmed him under a scorching June sun. And the next day he got laid out all peaceful-like in the parlor. People came from miles around to see the man and witness the most expensive funeral in the history of Billings Montana.

But probably the shrewdest thing I pulled off was I talked the woman into a side-venture. "Look," I said. "Big Lou was a showman. He'd want to go out of this life the same way he lived it." That always was a good line. And I talked her into a fifty-fifty proposition. We'd charge a dollar a head to non-circus folk to file-by and view Big Lou in his golden crasket. That same dollar also got your picture taken next to the man. To add some nostalgia to the photo I placed silver dollars on Big Lou's eyes to give the photo that old-timey feel.

And when all was said and done the crasket got hauled in a horse-drawn wagon the two-mile distance to the cemetery. People lined the streets like it was a Fourth of July parade. Big Lou must of been a good man cuz there wasn't a dry eye the entre route.

Men tipped their hats. Women held their babies. Babies blew kisses. It was a very humbling event.

Now I don't want you to think I was a flimflam man or nothing like that. Shrewd – yes. Flimflam – no. If a poor widow woman woulda come into my office that same day I woulda given her a fifty dollar funeral and the shirt off my back. But in business you got to be flexible with an eye on profit if you wantta make it in this hard knock world of ours. Truth is that circus woman would of squandered her inheritance if she hadn't spent it on the funeral-of-all-funerals. At least thata way Big Lou got a big sendoff and a bit of immortality. In Billings. Anyways.

My whole point to the story is this. When I ran the funeral home for those four months I sacrificed my education to take care of my brother and the business and pay the bills. I worked my tail off. And I took in over six thousand dollars. When Henry ran it the year after he come back to work he only took in two thousand. So you tell me. Who was the better businessman?

Ever since I decided working with dead people wasn't for me I have often wondered how much of my decision to leave Billings had more to do with a need to be self-reliant. Of taking control of life on my own terms without an older brother getting in the way. What the law today calls being emancipated as a minor. I got a glimpse of that when I was fifteen and what I saw I liked. Freedom. Independence. Self-determination. There's nothing like those things to keep a young man looking forward to what lays ahead. It's the same sorts of things that motivate us all as we go through life. And I suppose it's the same sorts of things that make us wantta take a walk on the moon or go running with the horses.

50

Above the aspens and north beyond Sage Creek, the boy followed the same worn trail meandering to the mountaintop that he had taken on six previous occasions, although the trail had lost some of its familiarity. After all, on one of those outings he rode unconscious and backwards; the other five were one-way downhill since the Beechcraft had ferried him up. Regardless, the trail pocked with hoofprints and the horse he rode, a gray appaloosa, seemed to know the way. Ever since they left Bopwadesh Hill, the horse had taken command. The boy rode slack on the reins while falling in and out of consciousness. Perhaps the meadow on top churned the horse's imagination and kept the creature's internal compass pointing toward clover. In any case, the farther up the mountain they went, the more surefooted the horse became much to the boy's relief, for the boy was in no shape to rely on his mental acuity or be demanding of the horse. Letting the horse take control suited the boy fine. Just fine.

When they reached the western edge of the great meadow, they heard multiple gunshots from off in the distance below. The horse stirred, growling a low nicker. The boy had always suspected that Hayyel, given a worst-case scenario, would sacrifice himself rather than give up his whereabouts, and he halted the horse and took off his hat in a moment of silence. Little else the boy could offer up as he knew the posse would soon be on his trail and moving at a much faster clip than he could muster given his condition. The logical first night's hideout, Penn's cabin, would be reachable before sunset and, no doubt, the place the posse planned to capture him.

The boy had devised a plan to evade his pursuers but recognized it might not work, let alone ever get implemented, given the slow crawl of the appaloosa. Realizing this, he heeled the horse and the horse jerked forward into a brisk canter. Every bounce hurt and the boy moaned in pain. Remaining conscience would be difficult at best. Still, he pressed on in spite of the injuries. The nose continued to throb and the upper lip puffed where it split and the missing teeth gaped. The contusions and cuts on the cheeks seemed less painful but still agonized. The one good eye, the right one, opened wide but the other eye remained welded shut. What preoccupied the boy's suffering, however, were the ribs where Lieutenant Mullin had kicked him while he lay unconscious in the meadow.

Now, with the jerking about from the cantering, the boy could no longer cope with the pain and he halted the horse and vomited. He wiped off his mouth and took a swig of water from the canteen, and decided to cut a leather strap off the saddle and clench it in his teeth. When the pain got bad, really bad, he would bite down hard and endure. The leather tasted salty and caused him to gag but he knew the only way not to cry out would be by biting on the strap. He heeled the horse into a full gallop, hoping the faster gait would be smoother, and bit down hard on the strap to the point where his jaw muscles ached, and pressed on.

When he reached the spot by the watering hole, the mustangs had re-congregated and seemed oblivious to his presence. Why they refused to scatter back into the woods remained a mystery and the boy assumed it had to do with a single rider not being perceived as a threat. He dismounted and scoured the woods next to the meadow and found his Winchester where he remembered the Lieutenant tossed it. He wiped down the barrel and checked its sights and except for some nicks on the stock, the weapon appeared to be in working condition. He slid it under the bedroll tied to the back of the saddle and remounted, then spun the horse around and broke past the bend in the trees, following the tree line to Penn's cabin and making sure their tracks remained visible.

Once they reached the cabin, the boy corralled the horse and threw the saddlebag with the jerky, matches, and ammunition over a shoulder. Over the other shoulder draped the canteen and the binoculars. He slid the rifle out from underneath the bedroll, un-cinched the saddle, and manhandled the saddle with its blanket over the fence railing, allowing it to become visible from down the meadow's approach. A few minutes later, he walked a sandstone outcrop to the cliff behind the cabin and scaled down its face to the rock canyon below. From there he headed along a rocky coulee until the coulee became a water-filled creek and the downstream water ran too deep and fast to ford. He scaled back up the adjoining cliff, checked his position relative to the cabin, and guessed his location to be a mile southeast.

The sun lay low on the horizon and less than an hour of light remained. Once nightfall came, the boy's trek to the west would rely on pure dead reckoning as the moon's lunar phase played out of sync with the timing of his plan. Hiking through the meadow, he came upon a climbable boulder and decided to scope the meadow's valley to check for the location of the posse before it got dark. Within seconds, he sighted the men surrounding the cabin. He thought he recognized the Sheriff hovering to the rear. Three other figures, presumably deputies, approached the cabin on foot carrying their revolvers high in the air. And for the first time since before the girl's death, the boy smiled. His plan was working. He had circled around his pursuers and left no tracks to give them the slightest inkling which direction he went or guess what he had formulated the minute he and Hayyel rode away from the PMRC. He slid down the boulder and picked up his pace. His ribs still hurt but by focusing on the rage over his friends' deaths, the ribs would hurt less as his destination neared. Soon, off in the distance he spied Black Mesa and knew that with a little bit of luck and a lot of fortitude, he would be back through the gap by daybreak. He knew if the Lieutenant had not left, the man would be enjoying a cigarette on the front porch of the big house like every morning at sunrise, and that is when he would kill him.

51

When daylight's first rays broke over the mountain's shoulders, the boy was already climbing Black Mesa's bench. Once on top, he walked the rocky flats to the southwest and to where the mesa dropped-off. He gazed through the shadow of the mesa, toward the big house, and realized he had reached his destination on time. The temperature had dropped to a crisp chill overnight and the occupant in the house had been burning wood in the potbellied stove. The smoke plumed high beyond the mesa and drifted off to the east. Lights glared inside and the boy felt a sense of relief. He was relieved to know he had come all that way in such harsh conditions and the Lieutenant was there, inside the house. He thought about laying flat on his belly for fear of being seen but came to the conclusion it made no difference if the Lieutenant saw him or not. By the time the Lieutenant caught a glimpse of him, if at all, the man would be dead. The boy was that sure of his targeting skills.

He removed the weighty saddlebag and canteen from his sore shoulders and laid them a few feet away but kept the binoculars handy. He knelt in a three-point stance, and for a minute checked and re-checked the rifle, convincing himself he had enough ammunition to get the job done—two cartridges in the clip plus one in the chamber. He guessed the total distance to the porch to be less than five hundred feet and, with the sun at his back, knew the shot or shots from his vantage would be easy. He adjusted the aperture to take into account the slight direction of the wind and the downward angle. Then, he practiced taking the shot, raising the bolt-action lever up and back, ejecting the cartridge, thrusting the bolt forward and down, and firing again: bolt up & back, eject, bolt forward & down, squeeze.

It had been nearly twenty-four hours since he had slept and his body was telling him he had pushed it as far and as fast as it could go. He had eaten some jerky on the run once he cleared the gap but hunger pangs had set in again, and a bout of diarrhea halfway down the mountain left him famished and dehydrated and slightly lightheaded. But with his adrenalin elevated, his ribs hurt less and the once swollen shut left eye was beginning to see again. The right eye, his targeting eye, had cleared up.

All night long, he had been playing the kill shot over-and-over in his mind. Whether to take aim at the Lieutenant's heart or pick the man apart one limb at a time had kept him coherent and angry—the sort of dark brew needed to keep moving. Now that he had reached his destination, he had yet to decide which manner of killing he preferred. The spare time gave him the opportunity to think things through.

He had heard the story of the mustangs that got cornered on top of the mesa and chose death over capture, and of Old White's fabled return, to watch the herd slaughtered from the very spot where he now stood. Once again, he felt the strong tie to the white horse. As he thought on these things, he began to wonder why he ever got involved in such a despicable scheme as killing horses in the first place. Perhaps the exhaustion had re-awakened his conscience but he felt ashamed. And as he readied for the Lieutenant to walk out on the front porch, he began to sob. What had he done? Why had he killed so many noble creatures? There had been far too much death the past few days and too little time to remember the dead. He yearned for everyone to be alive again, even the horses he never knew like the ones that had died there on the mesa. If he could just go back in time and start over he would, but he could not.

Within a few minutes, the door opened and the Lieutenant stepped out on the porch, cigarette in-hand the way he always did this time of day. The man leaned against a cedar beam, kicked a leg up on the railing and inhaled on the cigarette. It was as though nothing had changed in his world, at least based on the nonchalant body language. Life went on at the PMRC. The Lieutenant gazed lazily at the empty stockades, pleased with himself. He delicately pulled loose some tobacco from his tongue and flicked the bits in the air. Then, he exhaled blowing the smoke skyward.

It was all the boy needed to see. He laid down the binoculars, livid, and seized the rifle and took a long deliberate aim. That's when he felt the presence lurking over his shoulder, sighting in the target with him and whispering in his ear. "Always aim straight and true. Never rush the moment. When you're finished, savor what you've done."

The boy squeezed the trigger. The Lieutenant jerked and swatted at his left shoulder as though stung by a wasp. "That one's for Sully," the boy whispered. *Bolt up & back, eject, bolt forward & down, squeeze*. The man jerked again, this time swatting his right shoulder. When the Lieutenant realized something was terribly wrong, he stood up pressing his body against the railing for support. He began teetering forward. "That one's for Bob," the boy whispered again. *Bolt up & back, eject, bolt forward & down, squeeze*. This time the Lieutenant grabbed his chest. Blood exploded out his back. He heeled two steps, collapsing backward with his head crashing down on the porch planks. The boy stood up and pounded his heart. "And that one's for Hayyel, you piece of shit," he yelled.

52

The day the horses fled into the woods and escaped the PMRC crew, the white horse led them to the far side of the mountain. There, they waited until nightfall before returning. The watering hole near Penn's cabin had always been the herd's favorite, and the rich land surrounding the water yielded the most succulent meadow grasses. The site also served as the epicenter of their mating rituals. This summer proved no differently, and the herd's instinct to procreate overpowered their latent fear of the two-legged predator. Hence, they returned that night to copulate in a frenzied orgy under a crescent moon, oblivious to danger. A few months later, before the first snowfall could overtake them, they would migrate back to the harsh river basin eight thousand feet below. With a mild winter and some good fortune, by the next summer fifteen foals would join their ranks. Within four years, their numbers would double.

When light broke on the second day after his return to the herd, the white horse stood alone on the meadow's crest surveying his harem, soaking in the sun, and relishing all that he had accomplished. Instinct told him the herd was now safe and his job finished. It had been over ten weeks since he wandered to the hillside with the dancing horse manes and learned of man's ways. Now death beckoned again. It was time to relinquish his crown to one of the young stallions, for unlike humans who receive grandiose retirement sendoffs, he expected nothing and received nothing for all that he had done.

For the past day he had been feeling weak from the gunshot wound to the shoulder sustained near the Crow reservation. When the bullet struck, he had slipped backward and fallen down the snow packed slope and into the creek. The raging waters from the runoff carried him downstream. Where the creek pooled he managed to swim to a nearby bank, but once on land the leg could not bear weight, so he returned to the icy water. He remained buoyed by the stream while the water performed its therapeutic miracle. In time, he felt well enough to reunite with his herd but they had returned to the mountaintop, void of his leadership and unaware of the danger he had seen firsthand. When he caught up to them, he caught up just in time to challenge Judas.

Now his shoulder throbbed painfully and the lead fragments that lodged against his bone had infected the surrounding tissues. The entry hole that had once healed over festered oozing pus. The young bachelors had noticed the smell of the rotting flesh and muscle and would soon be challenging him for leadership. Best to abdicate now without a fight. Best to move on.

Moreover, if horses do ponder such heady matters as death, the white horse thought the time right to return his decaying body back to mother earth and complete the circle of life. With his demise inevitable, he limped away without ceremony and without looking back, and sauntered to the north and into the woods. Dust to dust, even for horses.

53

By the time the boy cleared the top of the gap, the sun had risen high enough to strike his eyes and blind his escape route. Rather than risk stumbling headlong into the posse, he moved south along the cliff and in the shadows, where he suspected the Sheriff and deputies would not search. The cliffs lay three thousand feet below Penn's cabin and circled around the mountain in a giant U. To the north the mountain stair stepped to a lower elevation along twenty miles of rolling foothills before yielding to the stark tor outcrops of gray gypsum. The cliffs, too, eventually melted into the mountain's foothills, about where the Crow reservation began and where Hayyel's cabin hid in its canyon. The top of the cliffs provided a flat and continuous surface for passable hiking and averted the strenuous ascent over the crest of Pryor Mountain. It would take longer to reach Hayyel's cabin, however. Given the terrain and his physical condition, the boy guessed the entire journey at four days.

From the cliff's southern apex and off in the distance, the boy could see the small farming community of Lovell, Wyoming, and the crisscrossed pattern of green irrigated fields. Farther up, the Bighorn River snaked its way south out of the canyon and disappeared into a sterile basin of gypsum and sandstone that cut through eons of earth's crust. There, the land streaked horizontal in mounds of red and orange and white and gray. Billions of years carved out foot-by-foot in layers of slow-motion history. The boy remembered his geology studies and knew the meaning of the colors. Each color corresponded to one of earth's epochs with each epoch equating to hundreds of millions of years. Even as he trekked along the top of the cliff, he couldn't help but marvel at the land. Seventeen years of life meant nothing relative to the unfathomable scale of earth's age.

He remembered his teacher explaining how if earth's time scale got condensed to twenty-four hours, man would have arrived in the twenty-third hour, fifty-ninth minute, and fifty-ninth second. As he pondered these things, it struck him how insignificant man was within that last second of time or how brilliant someone or something was in preparing all this for man. It was rare for the boy to think on these things because years earlier he convinced himself life was just an accident and that man spawned from the sea as an insignificant land urchin. Now, thinking about how the Bighorn River had carved out the earth, he pondered the possibility of a far more grandiose scheme to life.

Likewise, the boy had never given much thought to how it felt to be hunted like an animal. That is, until now. He despised the idea that the law had labeled him a dangerous fugitive yet, he understood. He understood how killing a person, regardless of the justification, was wrong; that men devised laws to condemn killers and that civilization could not survive on lawlessness. The fact he had murder on his hands put him in a bad way. Still, he felt little remorse or regret over what he had done. It was as Henry told him years earlier, 'There are good people and bad people in the world. The good deserve to live. The bad deserve to die.' Clearly, the Captain and Lieutenant deserved to die, the boy thought. Likewise, with both men dead the mustangs would thrive and multiply on Pryor Mountain.

He wondered what Sheriff John Toms thought of what he did and that consternation upset him. A week earlier the Sheriff and Martha invited him for supper and asked him to think about going back to school, getting his diploma, and moving to Laurel to work as a deputy. Might as well forget about becoming a deputy, he told himself. It'll never happen. Worse, he knew the Sheriff was required to hunt him down and bring him to justice. *But would the man use lethal force to get the job done?*

All these things ran through the boy's troubled mind as he hiked the cliff in his heightened state of exhaustion. Along the way, he forced himself to stop by a waterfall and refill the canteen and wash his face and hands. The cool water felt invigorating and he wanted to relax longer and soak in a nearby stream, but knew he needed to press on. Until he reached the safety of the cabin, he could get ambushed almost anywhere. Best to move on.

By midday the boy had covered over ten miles along the cliffs and had trekked beyond the southern loop of the U. The temperature warmed up enough where he began dripping sweat along the eastern wall where the rock captured the sunlight and the heat radiated on both sides of his face. With the sun taking its toll, he knew he could not go any further.

He came upon a small grotto-like fissure carved out by the river when the river elevated four thousand feet higher eons before. The fissure's low-profile setback went almost unnoticed from the cliff's trail. He discovered it when an eagle soared overhead and he followed the bird's trajectory to its nest above the entrance. Once the boy climbed to the location, he knew this would be the ideal hideout to spend the night. The place hid from the eyes of the law.

He scoured the floor for snakes and small animals but found none. When he checked the ceiling for bats and swallows, he discovered he had not been the first person who used the shallow cavern as a sanctuary. The ceiling coated thick with soot from the campfires of others who had traveled the same route centuries or millennia before. In a sense, the boy took solace in the revelation for he knew the 'others' had to have been the 'ancient ones' of local Indian folklore.

Like the weather the night before, the boy deduced the evening would be chilly, so with a final burst of energy he began to gather kindling from the surrounding hillside and stash wood next to where previous campfires once burned. While bringing in a second load, something on the ceiling caught his eye, and he brushed away the soot concealing the object and recognized the figure as an old Indian painting. He knew the painting classified as a pictograph, having seen such things at the park outside Billings. Out of curiosity, he took off his bandana and used it to dislodge more soot. When he finished cleaning an area six feet in diameter, he filled his hat with water that had pooled at the back of the grotto, and splattered it on the ceiling until the ceiling could no longer absorb anymore liquid and the water began dripping to the floor. Unexpectedly, the sublime figures burst forth in distinct vibrant colors. The boy fell to his knees and gazed up at the imagery—a giant shaman running with horses. The horses were red and white and blue, all shapes and sizes, and numbered fifty in total. The shaman held a knife in one hand and in the other what appeared to be a scalp of a horse mane. Overwhelmed by the sight, the boy tucked up his saddlebag into a pillow and lay flat on the dirt floor where he could look up and marvel at the entire scene. It was as though Hayyel had reached beyond the grave to tell him everything was all right and that his spirit now soared with horses in heaven.

Perhaps at that moment, the boy came closest to appreciating how things that happen in the fifty-ninth second do not always happen by accident. It could explain why his own life had taken so many turns and why he was now lying in a shallow cave hiding from the law. Then, watching the shaman run with the horses, he fell fast asleep.

54

"What exactly do you mean, *he slipped away?*" The voice roared the question out and into the hospital hallway.

"Well, Captain, the lad simply slipped through our snare. That's what I mean."

"How could that be, Sheriff? You and your men were sure he'd be spending the night at Penn's cabin."

"Look. I don't like this anymore than you. It makes me look bad and this is an election year." The Sheriff paused to reflect on the situation. He turned to gaze out the hospital window. "But—"

"But, what?"

"I still don't understand. I know Billy Bartell. I knew his parents. He comes from good stock. And—"

"Fiddly-dee, Sheriff. *Good stock*, you say? There's no such thing. Billy Bartell is a cold-blooded killer, plain and simple. He stole my entire savings. Gunned down my two best cowboys. Attempted to kill me. And came back and shot Lieutenant Mullin in an act of premeditated murder. So, tell me something, Sheriff. How will your constituents feel about a war hero being gunned down by a sniper and the killer escaping from your so-called snare without so much as a scratch?"

"And that's another thing I don't understand. Why would the boy come all the way back down the mountain to kill the Lieutenant if he already had your money? What was his rationale in doing that? Doesn't make sense."

"Sense? Of course, it makes sense. It was always about revenge. Revenge is one of the greatest motivations to kill in mankind's history. Revenge has been the mainstay of lustful killing since Helen of Troy. Obviously, when Lieutenant Mullin shot the half-breed it incensed the lad and sent him into a murderous frenzy. And if you hadn't noticed, he has a voracious temper."

"Never noticed that," the Sheriff responded. "So, are you still planning to head off to Oregon when you get out of here?"

"Yes. There is a large population of mustangs at Beatys Butte that must be eradicated. Oregon is where I will be." By now, the Captain was beginning to feel nauseated from the opiates given to dull his pain. While he had counted on the boy to shoot him in the head at the exact location of the steel plate, he did not anticipate the bullet shredding his forehead into mincemeat as it ricocheted round-and-round, bouncing between the inside of the bell gun's cone and the metal in his head. The skin graft from his thigh was taking but the thigh stung and no amount of pain relief could lessen the suffering. His head bandage seeped blood and the bedside nurse dabbed at it while he continued to rant. "So, what are you going to do, Sheriff? Let the lad run willy-nilly, free as a church mouse out there on the mountain?"

"Captain, there's not a whole lot I can do until Billy shows his head in public again. We'll keep APB's out for him. We'll keep wanted posters hung between here and Missoula, but I doubt he'll show."

"Won't show, you say? And just why not?"

"Because we think he fled to the Crow reservation to hole up there. If you didn't know it already, I've got no authority on Indian land."

The Captain rubbed his chin pondering the situation and then swatted at his nurse to move away. "You may not have the authority, but I do."

"What do you mean?"

"I'll tell you exactly what I mean. You ever heard of the Pinkertons?"

"Who hasn't?"

"Well, I figured you'd come up with some sort of malarkey like this and I made contingency plans."

"By hiring the Pinkertons?"

"That's right. These fellows know their business. When the J.B. Swift Company heard of my plight and Lieutenant Mullin's untimely demise, they offered to split the cost of the Pinkertons' services. Even the railroad offered a tidy sum of money, a bounty if you will, for the lad."

"Wait a minute. I thought the Pinkertons got put out of commission a few years back?"

"To a certain degree they did. But a few of their experienced hands hung around. And now they're on their way here, to Laurel, Montana. Big Jim Carson, Dapper Dan Rubottom, Frank Kline, and the famed tracker, Joe Lefors. They're calling themselves 'The Four Horsemen of the Apocalypse.'"

The Sheriff laughed without holding back.

"What's so funny?'

"I know who those men are. They were big names when I was a kid. They were involved in hunting down The-Hole-In-The-Wall Gang. *Holy Cow*. That was over thirty-five years ago. Lefors has to be in his seventies. Can he even ride a horse anymore?" The Sheriff chuckled after the question.

"I suspect horses may be used, but I also suspect my agents of death will use the latest twentieth century technology to help them capture their man."

"Like what?"

"Ah-h-h-h, now I have your attention. Don't I. First, they'll be employing my aeroplane spotter, T. Fenneus Johnson the Third of Denver, Colorado, to locate the boy. Then, they'll be communicating with him wirelessly via portable radio transmission and track him down. *Voila*. One less desperado in the world."

"And you think they're going to come all the way out here just to nab a seventeen-year-old boy who has yet to be indicted by the governor's office?"

"Oh, yes, indeed. The right amount of money has the most miraculous way of inducing the killer instinct. Plus, I expect the governor to put a bounty on the boy's head, soon. Very soon. Let me assure you, Sheriff, these Pinkerton men are as desperate as the lad, himself."

"Really? And why's that?"

"Besides the money, they have something to prove. They want to set right the Pinkerton name and show they still possess the mettle they had as younger men. Desperate men make the most ruthless hunters of criminals, Sheriff Toms. They will stop short of nothing to catch their prey. Don't expect the lad to walk away from this. My guess is he'll put up one hell of a fight and go out in a blaze of glory. His kind always do."

The Sheriff heard enough. He moved next to the bed and wrapped his hand tight around the Captain's throat. The nurse ducked out of the room. "Listen, you. If your people find Billy Bartell, they had better not harm a hair on his head. They'd better turn him over to me. *Alive*. There's something fishy here and I aim to find out what it is firsthand from the boy himself. Got it?"

The Captain nodded his head 'yes.'

55

The boy found the cabin after days of hiking. It lay at the floor of a narrow canyon where he remembered sighting it from the Beechcraft window. That is, once he found the canyon. The stark terrain twenty miles northeast of Pryor Mountain rolls with indistinguishable gypsum hills. Red clay flats spread out between the hills and where the two collide, dull plains grass and sage grow in convoluted kinship. The landscape looked the same in every direction and fooled the boy's sense of perspective. When, by pure happenstance, he stumbled upon the huge crack in the earth, he realized he had reached his destination. Below him, the oasis-like canyon ran bright green with cottonwoods and fjord-like meadows. A raging creek cut through the chasm and collided with boulders as the water coursed its way toward the Big Horn River. Less than two hundred feet across and one hundred feet in depth, the canyon made the perfect refuge from the constant winds and harsh conditions of the arid pre-foothills. It also made for the perfect lair.

The cabin butted up to a rock precipice facing south. Less than thirty feet separated the front door from the creek. White water raced around massive rocks with late snow runoff providing the source of the turbulence. Even from his angle standing above and looking down, the boy caught glimpses of trout dancing airborne over the rocks, presumably on their way to spawn. Watching all this, the boy realized he had somehow discovered an uninhabited Garden of Eden and that it lay in wait for his occupancy.

Within minutes, he found a worn goat trail that led down to the water. From there he rock-hopped across the creek and then walked upstream to a small corral with a shed that Hayyel used for packhorses. Farther up and around a slight bend in the canyon, the one room log cabin sat abandoned and in sore need of human occupancy. With the cabin squatty low and dug into the ground, at six-foot the boy stood a foot taller than the highest roofline elevation. New tin panels sandwiched over old post-size vegas and what once comprised the all-wood flat roof. Hayyel left extra panels lying about like loose change and the boy had to step over them to get to the front door. A perpetual remodeling had been taking place at the old cabin for some time. Inside, the room smelled musty. Cobwebs hung everywhere. The boy laid his belongs on a table and set about sprucing up the place. He propped open the two front shutter-windows to let light in since the cabin had no traditional glass windows, and began sweeping and dusting. Everything seemed in order including a potbellied stove and a homemade latrine with a porcelain bowl plopped underneath.

When he finished tidying up, the boy checked the shelves for provisions and found the place well stocked: assorted canned goods, mostly peaches, dried beans, rice, coffee, a box of .30-06 cartridges, and five gallons of kerosene for three lamps. There was enough food to outfit him for at least two or three months but not enough to make it through winter. He lit one of the lamps and got an even better look inside, and moved to a corner where books stacked waist high and included a menagerie of collectibles ranging from Shakespeare's plays to Greek tragedies to the writings of a French philosopher named Gabriel Marcel. Piled on top were two Sears & Roebuck catalogues much to the boy's relief.

A pair of wall-mounted fishing poles caught the boy's attention and, having earlier set his sights on a trout dinner, he took the poles along with a tackle box and landing net and went outside to sit by the creek. The flies had been handmade and he selected two and tied them onto ends of the casting lines. It seemed eerie that Hayyel's hands might have crafted the flies he was about to use and that he was now sitting there at the cabin alone, but he also knew his friend would have wanted it to be this way. He knew Hayyel wanted him to be safe. He tried not to think about the events that caused him to flee to the canyon or about Sully and Bob, but did sigh before casting the lines into the water and slow-reeled in the flies, first one line then the other. On the third cast he caught a seventeen-inch brown but released it. On the fourth, he reeled in a twenty-one-inch rainbow and guessed it weighed over three pounds; ample enough meat for both dinner and breakfast. He gutted and cleaned the fish and found some lard in an old coffee can and soon had trout frying on a skillet atop the stove. He captured some water in a bucket and set it to a boil, used some of it to hydrate the beans and rice, and set some aside for drinking. An hour later, he sat down at a table and ate a full meal, his first in days. The leftover rainbow trout never made it to breakfast.

Much later, he took one of the two cabin chairs, sat outside, and gazed up at the night sky. He wondered if blind luck steered him to the canyon that day or if it had somehow been ordained all along and coded within the mystery of the stars. He caught himself smiling again as the thought struck and shook his head in a capitulated but humored snort. Since when, he mused, was hiding out from the law either lucky or ordained? He leaned back in the chair, propping it against the doorframe, and kicked one boot on top of the other, tipping his hat over his eyes. Within seconds, he fell asleep, exhausted. That night the only thing causing the boy to stir was a rancid burp reeking of trout and beans and rice.

56

Within a week the boy had lay claim to everything half a mile above and below the cabin. Unlike the sandstone cliffs surrounding Pryor Mountain, the canyon's steep precipices had no caves or fissures to explore and consisted of shale and basalt. During his daily hikes an occasional raccoon or possum would greet the boy but, other than that, he had become bored with his surroundings and yearned for human companionship or anything that might break the monotony of his new monastic lifestyle. Cabin fever had struck. Even the boy's everyday staples of trout and beans and rice had lost their novelty. So, after a week of exploring and fishing and reading the two Sears & Roebuck catalogues front to back and visa-versa, he decided to leave the security of the canyon and venture above to hunt game—elk, deer, antelope, native sheep—and explore new territory.

Once on higher ground, the land seemed dryer and more desolate than he remembered. There had been no rain the past seven days and the wild plains grasses had turned yellowish-brown; the sage always looked thirsty but, after a week without water, seemed even more withered than normal. Hiking west, he decided to stay close to the canyon's rim and not risk getting lost. Every fifty yards or so he would peek over the edge to maintain his bearings but when he reached where his canyon explorations had ended a few days before, he refused to go any further. He stopped and stood on his tiptoes and surveyed the area and concluded that hiking a mile in any direction would yield the same result—ugly barren land without game. He gazed to his left and could see the foothills rising in gradual steps with each step darker green all the way up the backside of the mountain. To his right the terrain shimmered in a hazy miasma. What little moisture remained in the ground evaporated into mirage after mirage all the way north to

Billings and Laurel to the northwest. With gray and red dust clouds kicking up in the distance, he wondered how anything could survive the extreme daytime heat without water. About the moment he concluded there was little motivation to go any farther and to return to the cabin, he noticed buzzards circling to the south a few hundred yards away. Curious, he followed the birds' flight to check out the commotion. As he approached the location, he spotted an animal lying on its side and semi-conscious. The animal lay a few feet short of its intended objective, a basin of water. The creature panted in short staccato bursts; its tongue unraveled on hot dusty sand. But a giant sage blocked the boy's full line of sight and it wasn't until he circled around the sage that he recognized the animal as the white horse, the one known as Remliel. Taken aback and bewildered by the spectacle of this particular mustang being near death, a thousand thoughts crossed the boy's mind. *How had the horse gotten there? Why had it picked this spot to die? Why did their paths keep crossing?*

The horse's shoulder had abscessed where it had been shot and the smell permeated the air. It seemed obvious the poor thing had become sick and wandered away from its herd to die the way mustangs in the wild do—alone. The boy approached the horse cautiously for fear of spooking or riling it into an attack. From ten feet away it became apparent the animal was in no shape to be combative or frightened.

The boy filled his hat with water from the basin and took it to the horse. The horse gulped it down along with five more hatfuls. With the sixth hatful, the boy mixed some red clay with water and pressed the antidote against the abscess. The rest of the water, including the water from his canteen, he rubbed over the horse's eyes and head.

"There, there, old fella," he said. "That's about all I can do for you here. You're gonna have to come with me if you wantta get any better. And that means you're gonna have to trust me and I don't blame you one bit you if you can't. After all, I am the one that did this to you. But if you decide to come along, I promise I'll never hurt you again. Ever. You and me, we got too much history together. We got too much living to do. Come on now. Get yourself up." The boy unhitched his rifle strap and looped it around the horse's neck and yanked hard hollering, "*Get up.*"

The shout stirred the horse back to full consciousness and the creature shook its head. It sat up bewildered by everything and then began rocking itself back and forth. On the sixth or seventh rock, it had enough momentum to lurch to its knees and from that position to a full stand. For a minute the boy and the horse eyed each other from three feet. The boy said and did nothing but held tight to the strap. Finally, convinced the horse had accepted him, at least for the time being, he reached out and stroked it around the eyes again. "Come on, old fella. Let's get outta here. It's too darned hot."

The boy led the horse back to the canyon rim with the horse limping and the boy chatting nonstop. While the boy had been in dire need of companionship, he never dreamt it would come in the form of a wild mustang.

Once the horse corralled, the boy made a bed of grass and filled up the trough with fresh creek water, and withdrew to the cabin where he boiled water. He returned with his pocketknife sterilized, a bucket full of the germ-free water and soap and clean towels. The horse had once again collapsed on its side and when the boy washed its shoulder, it never flinched or complained. He cut open the abscess, drained it dry, and probed the wound with his fingers until he fished out two bullet fragments. When he finished, he flushed the lesion with the boiled water and re-washed the shoulder. Blood had pooled on the ground and the boy knew that without pressure applied to the gaping incision the horse might very well bleed to death. He withdrew to the cabin and returned with a blanket, and covered up the horse in anticipation of the cold evening. He packed new mud over the spot he had just cut on and laid on top of the horse to both keep the horse warm and apply pressure to the wound. The horse did nothing the entire time but shiver from the onset of fever. Its eyes remained closed.

"Don't you die on me, old fella. Already had everyone else die on me. Not you, too. *Hear?*"

By the time night arrived, the boy had fallen asleep on top of his horse. The horse had been awake for some time but did not stir for fear of losing the warmth of the boy. And they remained that way throughout the night while the stars mapped their fate and bad men plotted to kill them both.

57

Martha Toms had been waiting for her husband to walk through the door but fell asleep on the sofa sometime after midnight. When the latchkey turned, she awoke and dashed to the front door before John could cross the threshold.

"You're still awake," he said, expecting as much.

"No. Well, yes. I mean, I fell asleep on the couch but I couldn't go to bed. I'm just worried about—"

"*Billy*," he interrupted. "It's okay. I am, too."

"Did the Pinkerton men get off at the station?"

"Yes," he answered. "About forty-five minutes ago."

"Did you talk with them?"

"Yes."

"Are they still going to stay and chase after him?"

" I'm afraid so."

Martha clenched her fist in anger. "Damn it, John. Can't you stop them?"

"How?"

"I don't know how. Arrest them. Lock them up and—"

"And throw away the key?"

"Yes."

"I can't do that. They have every legal right to be here and do what they're going to do. Montana hasn't outlawed bounty hunters. Not yet, anyway."

"But the bounty—"

"Yesterday. Yesterday the governor set it at dead or alive. A thousand dollars either way. Add that to the thousand that's already been raised against the boy and I'm afraid he's worth more dead than alive."

"But can't you find Billy before those men do?"

"I'd sure like to but if he's hiding out on the reservation, I can't set foot in there."

"Then, why can they?"

"Because men like that don't always follow the letter of the law. Because they can sneak in and out before the tribe realizes what happened."

"Oh, John. Everything is so wrong." Martha threw herself into her husband's arms and sobbed. John embraced her and wanted to cry, too. "I know Billy didn't do all those horrible things," she said. "And if he did, there had to be a reason. I just know it."

"Martha, don't cry. I'm going to do everything I can to protect Isaac and Jennie's boy. Everything I can. I promise."

LVIII

My Pa used to take me to church with him when I was little.
Actually. He and Henry would go to the church service and I'd get
Shanghaied off to Sunday school. And I hated it. I think the whole
purpose behind the institution was to scare little kids before they
got old enough to think things through on their own. What I mean
is this. Outta one side of their mouth they'd preach how Jesus
loves you and by His grace we're all getting into heaven. Then
outta the other side of their mouth they'd preach how you'd better
believe in the Man and accept him or you'll be damned and go
straight to the eternal fires of hell. Now that's a lotta scare to put
on a child. Like having a loaded and cocked gun put to your head
and being asked 'Do you believe?' knowing if you say 'I'm not
sure' you're gonna get a bullet in the brain. So which is it? Either
the Man loves you or He doesn't. And if He doesn't why not?
What'd you do so bad in this life that ticked Him off and He
couldn't forgive you?

And how about all those folks born before Jesus? Who never
knew a lick about Him? They going to hell? And what about folks
like Gandhi and Buddha? Seemed like good people to me. They
believed in the hereafter. They going to hell too? And the Indians.
Good people all. They have their own ideas about heaven. And the
horses? Don't they have souls? Aren't they pure of heart? How
about the other animals of this world of ours? Seems to me the
only evil souls are those of man. Seems to me that heaven oughtta
be filled with the sweet and good creatures that lived on earth and
only an occasional human since us two-legged types are so
downright cruel to one another. Guess that's why when I was little

*I created my own idea of where you go when you die. I called it
'my Montana heaven.' And it belonged to me and whoever else I
could get in there. After all. In Sunday school they also preached
about God's house having many rooms. How about a room just for
Billy Bartell?*

*So I'm nine or ten years old and starting to have my doubts
about what they're feeding me at Sunday school. And my teacher
says to me, "Billy, you aren't listening to a word I'm saying. Is
there something wrong?"*

*"Yes, Ma'am, there is," I said. "My yellow Lab, Duke, just died
and I've been missing him something fierce."*

*Well now. That teacher got all pouty-faced sad and says back to
me all righteous-like, "I'm sorry, Billy, to hear of your loss.
There's a purpose in Duke's passing and that is to teach us
humility in death and the power of the Lord's will."*

*"Thank you, Ma'am," I lied since I had no earthly idea what
she meant by all that. "It's just that I won't get to see my dog
again for a long-long time."*

"What do you mean see him again?" she asks.

*"I mean, I won't get to see him again until I get into my
Montana heaven," I answered.*

*Well now. That woman cocks her head like she didn't hear me
quite right and says, "Billy, I'm not real sure what you mean by
your 'Montana heaven,' but I can assure you dogs can't go there.
First, they don't believe in Jesus. Second, they don't have souls.
And third, even if they did, they haven't been baptized."*

*Now that really upset me and I got angry. A little too angry. But
I was nine or ten and the woman didn't cut me any slack for being
a child. Anyways. I said back to her, "Look. My dog Duke is going
to heaven and I am gonna see him again."*

*Needless to say the woman didn't like my tone of voice and she
got real stern-like. "Billy. Listen and listen good," she says. "Dogs
aren't allowed in heaven."*

*"Oh, yeah?" I shouted. "In my Montana heaven there's dogs
and cats and all of the good animals that got loved here on earth.
There's only one animal not allowed and that's you cuz you just
got a one-way ticket to my Montana hell."*

You can imagine. The woman grabbed me by the ear and dragged me down the hall while I was yelling and screaming. She took a lot of glee in washing out my mouth with a bar of soap. But it was worth it. I would have eaten soap everyday if that's all it took to get sweet Duke into heaven.

Later Henry told me that he could hear the commotion all the way into the sanctuary. "Good," I told him. "I hope Jesus heard me too cuz he needs to get ready." "Ready for what?" Henry asked. "Ready for Duke," I said. "I'm bringing him through the Pearly Gates if the Man Upstairs allows it or not."

59

Two days after extracting the bullet fragments, the boy's horse continued to drift in and out of consciousness. The boy soon ascertained how the horse's recovery had as much to do with old age as the severity of the wound. After all, he had heard countless stories about Old White from the cowboys and Hayyel; he knew the horse had been living around Pryor Mountain since the early twenties. Yet, he also knew the horse would die if it continued lying on its side with a fever. Hence, on the third day the boy forced the horse to stand and begin its rehabilitation, old age or not.

At first, the process involved simple walks around the corral, twice-daily cleanings of the wound, and muscle massage. By the fifth day, the corral had grown too small and the horse required more exercise space than the repetitive loop next to the railing. The boy decided to open the fence and walk the horse upstream to where one of the narrow creek meadows lay abundant with grass and clover. There, he hobbled the horse's hind legs with rope and turned it loose and watched it devour everything edible and green. The horse's ravenous appetite was a good sign. It meant full recovery was near. It also meant the boy could cease his arduous routine of sickling stem grass twice a day and allow the horse to scavenge for food on its own.

One day, while the boy fished in the middle of the creek and while the horse gorged on the bank, the boy noticed the hobbling rope had slipped off. Like all animals that taste their first morsel of freedom, the horse took off. When the boy approached it on foot, the horse took off farther upstream. Every time the boy got near, the horse would saunter or scurry in the opposite direction, refusing to allow the boy within ten feet of where it stood. This cat-and-mouse game continued all afternoon and for almost a full mile to where the canyon narrowed and where little grass grew along the creek. Offended by the horse's behavior, the boy gave up the pursuit, or at least gave the appearance of giving up. All the tricks he learned at Sheridan—avoiding eye contact, walking laterally and speaking in a soft calming manner—were ineffective. So, he decided to take a different tactic. *He ignored the horse altogether.*

He waded out into the creek, found a good-sized boulder, and lay down on his back with his hat cocked over his eyes to feign sleep. While the horse disliked being chased after, it hated the lack of attention even more. Sure enough, within thirty minutes it returned to the boy, wading through the water and nuzzling the lad. The boy sat up with a most satisfied grin. "Well, guess you missed me after all," he said. He stroked the horse on the ears and around the eyes and then looped some twine around its neck to let it know that it had been 're-captured,' and led it back to the corral.

The next day the boy turned the horse loose near the cabin, this time without the hobble, in a test of wills. Surprisingly, the horse seemed content grazing nearby without wandering away. Earlier, the boy had moved the table and a chair outside by the creek. He sat contentedly watching the horse eat while his boots kicked up on the table and he leaned back on the chair; a grass stem drooped from his mouth. Fully relaxed, the boy gazed downstream and at the canyon walls and at the blue sky overhead and, for the second time since escaping to Hayyel's compound, realized how lucky he had been. The place percolated with earth's rare bounties and could sustain him and the horse until winter set in. Even now, he told himself, if he were to become captured or killed, he could confidently state he had come closest to experiencing inner peace than at any other time in his short lifespan.

As he watched the horse grazing, it occurred to him that he had yet to name it. He disliked the old timer's moniker 'Old White' and had never connected with the Crow word 'Remliel.' After all, he reminded himself, he was a cowboy, not an Indian. He pondered over suitable names and could concoct nothing that seemed satisfying or possessed any real significance. The horse had responded to 'Fella' and 'Old Fella,' names that conveyed nothing noteworthy. To the boy those names made about as much sense as naming a newborn 'Little Tike' or 'Young-un.' But since the horse recognized few human words, the boy decided to stick with what he brought to the dance, so to speak. "Come here, *Old Fella*," he blurted, patting his thigh in a come-hither patter.

The horse looked up from gnawing on grass and, with cat-like haughtiness, meandered to where the boy sat, and began sniffing on the lad. The boy reciprocated, hugging on the horse. "You and me," the boy whispered, "we're good friends. Ain't we, Old Fella?" The horse nuzzled the boy even more and the boy laid his head against the horse's cheek and fed it the grass stem that had been dangling from his mouth.

Indeed, the boy and his horse had found peace and friendship in the quiet canyon valley that once belonged to Hayyel Gabriel.

60

The new tin roof had been Hayyel's way of keeping melting ice from dripping through the loose vega slats. Hayyel hated a cold muddied cabin floor in the spring. But in the late summer the tin served a far different purpose. Tin reflected the intense sunlight and helped keep the dugout cabin cool. It also served as a beacon to anything flying overhead like the Beechcraft Staggerwing aircraft searching for the boy.

When the plane buzzed the cabin on the first pass, the boy had been brushing his horse in the corral. He looked up and saw the yellow bird streak by from an altitude of less than two hundred feet with T.F.'s face pressed against the cockpit side window. The boy's first impulse was to wave to his old acquaintance but when he saw the sneer on T.F.'s face, the reality of the situation sunk in—*the man was out to nab him*. Although the boy had no idea who might have paid for T.F.'s services, he did know T.F. skimming close to the ground had nothing to do with a casual Sunday jaunt out of Denver. The man flew for money. As far as the boy knew, the Sheriff could have hired him but even that prospect seemed unlikely. Even if the Sheriff knew where he holed up, state law had no recourse on Crow land. Therefore, the boy deduced T.F. must be working with a bounty hunter or hunters, and a hefty reward placed on his head, at least hefty enough to warrant the use of the Beechcraft. By the time the plane circled back, the boy had already sprinted for the cabin to retrieve the rifle and binoculars. He snapped in the clip and pocketed a handful of cartridges, and then looked across to the south rim of the canyon. There was no time to rock-hop over the creek and climb the goat trail to escape. If riders were approaching, they would be coming up from the south. *Best to flee in the opposite direction.*

The boy grabbed hold of the rock wall behind the cabin and began scaling the narrow breaks in the precipice. He managed to pull himself up on the rim just as T.F. zoomed by a third time. Knowing T.F.'s operational procedure all too well—locate prey, radio in the location, capture and kill—his heart raced fearing the inevitable. In this case, the boy had no clue as to whom T.F. might be radioing but figured it to be just about anyone thirsty for blood money.

When T.F. swooped by a fourth time, the craft's propellers almost mowed down the boy. The boy hit the ground and let the plane pass overhead, then jumped back up into a three-point stance. As the plane banked, the boy took aim and fired a shot but at that distance and speed there was no telling if he hit anything. Fortunately, T.F. retreated southwest toward the mountain. The boy watched all this through the binoculars. He also watched the plane tip its wings back-and-forth as if signaling to someone below. That worried him even more. He sprinted to higher ground and glassed the area a mile away and spotted what he had been dreading for weeks—a posse. The lead rider already had a rifle drawn.

The boy knew if he took off on foot they would run him down. Crossing over to the north side of the canyon where he stood, however, would not be easy. To do so, the riders would have to make a choice. Either they could circle around the rim to the west, losing an hour or more of valuable time, or they could descend straight into the canyon via the goat trail, ford the creek, and climb out following the old road a half-mile east and downstream. All this predicated on T.F. not returning. If T.F. returned as a spotter and stayed out of rifle range, the boy's every move could be communicated to the ground. Running seemed futile. He glassed the men again and counted four riders. He searched for the aircraft. It had disappeared. What to do now?

A horse whinny echoed up the canyon and caught the boy off guard. In his haste, he had forgotten about the horse. He turned and watched the creature pace in the corral. If he deserted the horse, it would be shot or slaughtered or starve in its hold. He promised that no harm would ever befall it again. Abandonment was unthinkable.

He re-scoped the four men as they galloped toward the south rim and guessed he still had a few minutes. Frantic, he climbed back down the precipice. His one option with the horse lay to the east, down the canyon and up through the old abandoned road that headed northwest. Together, they would race toward Laurel and the rail terminus where he would catch a train to freedom.

Twenty feet from the canyon floor, the boy knew time was running out and he jumped the rest of the way, twisting his ankle in the fall. He ignored the pain, grabbed the new rope hackamore and the canteen from the cabin, and then fast-limped to the corral. The four men would soon be spotting him from the south rim and taking pot shots. At that short distance, he and the horse would be easy targets. The further down the canyon they could flee the better chance for drawing the men into pursuit. If the men pursued, there would be no gunplay. It would boil down to a horserace. Only problem, the boy's horse had never been ridden and the horse's shoulder hadn't time to heal.

When he reached the corral, the horse knew something was afoul and trotted back and forth, bumping up against the corral rails. Its tail stood vertical from fright. The boy tried calming it. "Look, Old Fella," he pled, ripping down railing as he spoke, "I need your help. You and me, we got a fly like the wind from here. We got a give them bad men on top the race of a lifetime. Okay, Fella? Can you do this for me?"

The horse pawed the ground. It sensed danger the way all wild animals do when cornered by a predator. Its nostrils flared and its head tossed ready. When the boy slipped the hackamore over its muzzle and threw himself on top, bareback, yelling *giddyup*, the horse's instincts took over. It bolted out the corral and raced down the canyon. The boy leaned forward and held on.

As the boy suspected, the first rider had already dismounted at the edge of the rim and spotted him on the horse. Two other riders came next and stood looking over their mounts to the canyon floor. The rider named Lefors, the most experienced tracker of the lot, had been towing the packhorse with the radio; he was the last to arrive at the scene. "If you got a shot, you'd better take it now," he hollered.

The first rider had already taken aim but the twists in the canyon and the boy's speed on the horse gave him little opportunity to pull the trigger. "Damn it all," he yelled, kicking the ground. He looked down at the canyon floor and over at the opposite rim. "We know he's got to go north. How the hell do we get over there?"

Lefors turned his horse to the west and craned his head to look upstream. "T.F. said there's a narrow break back up yonder 'bout a hundred yards. We go down it, cross the creek, and follow the kid's trail. Best guess the kid knows a way out. When we get him on open range, we take him down."

The one called Jimmy spoke up. "The kid's horse is too fast. We'll never catch him."

"Why the hell did T.F. hightail?" the first rider asked.

"Said the kid put one through the canopy."

The third rider, the young one named Kline, spat some chaw and then wiped his mouth dry with the back of his glove. He stewed angry. "Guess old T.F. is nothin' but a coward in that chick-yeller aeroplane a his. The son-o-bitch gets paid top dollar. Now he's gone runnin' home just cuz the kid got off a lucky shot." He turned to Lefors steely-eyed. "You get him on that there radio and tell him that I will personally kick his ass to high noon if he don't come back pronto."

The first rider was still standing next to the canyon's rim. After he watched the boy disappear, he turned to look at his partners. Exhaustion reflected off his weathered face. For over a week they had been riding hard while hunting the boy down in the wilds, all this in searing heat and wind, and without letup. Even as a younger man, the grueling ordeal would have worn him ragged. Now, his face showed all of the hard-lived sixty years he had been struggling on earth and he had enough. To have come all that way and have the boy slip away epitomized many frustrations of late including the indictment of his employer. The Pinkerton organization was floundering and on its last leg. Collecting the pension and retiring to the fishing cabin in northern Minnesota never seemed so attractive. "Hell, boys. You don't get it do you?"

he asked. "You don't really want T.F. coming back here. Not really. Him coming back is our final curtain."

"What are you talking about, Dan?" Lefors asked.

"Tell you what I'm talking about. Your tracking days are as good as over. So are yours and yours," he said pointing to the two other riders, "and so are mine. They only hired us because they haven't figured it out yet. Need a desperado hunted down? You hire a Pinkerton man, right? *Wrong.* It don't work like that anymore. That aeroplane can take out the boy without us. That's just the way it is. This twentieth century of ours, it's passed us by. They don't need our kind. Problem is we got us a city-boy pilot that doesn't know jack shit what he's doing when it comes to hunting down the criminal element." He moved closer to his friend Lefors and placed his hand on the old man's saddle horn. "Know what? We're all getting too up in years for this. The heat. The flies. And my back hurts something awful. So, what say you we all go back to town and put our boots up and drink us a cold one? Maybe it's best to let our pilot take down the kid. Hell, we'll still collect our share regardless who does the deed."

Lefors understood. "Where are the grenades?" he asked.

"Back at the PMRC camp," the one named Kline answered.

"Hells, bells," Jimmy said. "I don't trust T.F. to do squat. Lefors, you radio chicken-yeller. Tell him to load up that box of grenades and come pick me up. Lot easier to blow the kid and his horse to Kingdom Come than chase after 'em with guns blazing. Money is just as green with an aerial grenade as an earthbound bullet. Besides. That white horse runs like a god damned ghost."

61

The boy and his horse had been riding hard for over two hours. Earlier, when they climbed out of the canyon, they raced headlong into the vast gypsum tors and red clay flats that stretched endlessly about. Just as the boy guessed a few weeks earlier, the land swept the same in every direction—bleak and desolate and barren. Occasionally, he would glance down at the horse's hooves as they galloped through the soft clay. To the rear, a telltale line of pocked hoof prints broadcast their escape route. The hoof prints confirmed what even the most novice bounty hunter would suspect: the boy and his horse were heading north toward the rail yard in Laurel. The boy's tactical advantage lay with the speed of the horse and the horse's performance was flawless. More than once the boy whispered in his mount's ear, "Thank you, Old Fella."

Now, the terrain began easing upward into rolling grass knolls. The boy guessed it was the beginning of the Yellowstone River valley or the backside of the river's hilly basin. A few miles beyond the hills, the river valley would spread out with Laurel lying on the other side. The boy glanced over his shoulder for the tenth time and detected no one chasing after them. No dust kicked up from riders and their horses, or engine droned from a skyborne aircraft.

When they reached the first grassy upslope, the boy halted the horse and glassed the land south for movement. Nothing stirred and he could not understand what happened to the bounty hunters. Certainly, they hadn't given up, he thought. He dismounted and drank from the canteen and checked the horse's shoulder. The wound had opened up but little blood seeped out, much to his surprise. It meant the horse still had the stamina to carry him the remaining distance. But the horse needed water, so he began scouring the area for a spring or creek. Up ahead he spotted a working windmill with a water trough for cattle. He decided to walk the horse to the trough and keep an eye peeled for anything that moved. In this case, 'anything' meant anything hinting of man or bad men on horseback or flying machines. He knew this lull was just that, a temporary reprieve. Anyone who had taken the time to find him in the canyon in the daytime heat, expending all that energy on the dry side of the mountain, had the patience to track him down to the lush side of the Yellowstone River valley.

When they reached the trough, the boy re-checked the horse's shoulder and then filled his hat with cool water to wipe away the salt build-up on the horse's withers and flanks. The horse's chest coated deep white in ringed bands of crystalline salt and he washed down as much as he could. Five minutes into the rest, the horse's head jerk-raised, dripping water from its muzzle. Its ears flipped back. The boy turned around and saw nothing. He raised the binoculars to gaze toward the southern horizon and spotted the yellow bird close to the ground following their tracks. "Shit," the boy muttered. He slid the rifle off his shoulder and counted his cartridges. Five bullets made up the arsenal. As the craft drew nearer, T.F. spotted them by the windmill and yanked back hard on the steering yoke to gain altitude and stay out of sniper range. The boy had already taken aim but backed off when the craft banked and circled like a shark from a safe distance.

The boy spoke to his horse as if the creature understood the situation. "I'm guessing we got a few more miles ahead of us, Old Fella. Hang in there. We won't have an easy go of it." He grabbed hold of the horse's mane and pulled himself back on, and then heeled the horse in the flanks. They took off heading in the direction of the grassy-covered hill a quarter of a mile away. As soon as they cleared the crest, the Beechcraft came after them, swooping low to the ground while using the hill to hide the angle of attack. When the boy and horse passed midway down the backside of the hill, the plane zoomed over the crest in pursuit at an elevation of less than a hundred feet. The craft swooped even lower as it neared its target, hugging the ground, and veered toward the coulee the boy and the horse had just crossed. When the craft roared overhead, the boy yanked the reins right. A few seconds later, an explosion shook the ground. The concussion startled the horse and it came to a stiff-legged halt hitching the boy up its neck. The boy felt something warm trickle down his cheek. He touched the spot and came up with blood. The concussion had shattered an eardrum. He twirled around looking for the Beechcraft but it had dived over the next hill. T.F.'s hide-and-seek strategy was working. The boy couldn't get off a shot.

The boy re-heeled the horse and they raced down the coulee perpendicular to their previous heading and counter to what the boy presumed to be the Beechcraft's next approach. The boy knew they could neither remain a stationary target nor head in the same predictable direction by going uphill. Sure enough, when T.F. skimmed the hill on the return pass expecting to find the boy in the same vicinity, his target had slipped two hundred yards downstream. The speedy Beechcraft couldn't react and vanished over the crest of the first hill, once again denying the boy a clear shot. The boy, however, changed direction again and chased up the hill after the craft, pulling out his rifle while on the run.

By staying low on the horizon, T.F. had no idea where the boy and the horse now scampered. The boy guessed the Beechcraft's location by the roar of the throttled engine. When the craft returned hugging the crest, the landing gear almost knocked the boy off the horse. The boy swivel-turned and fired off two shots. The first one struck the lower fuselage and a fuel tank. The second one struck something metallic and ignited a spark. Within seconds, flames shot from the plane's belly. At that point, the boy expected T.F. to find a pasture to land the craft but the pilot refused to yield and began to circle back around.

"Damn, you," the boy shouted, shaking his fist at the craft.

Unbeknownst to the boy, inside the cockpit Jimmy had pulled out a revolver and tucked its barrel into the back of T.F.'s head. "We're going back to get the boy," he demanded.

"Are you insane? We're on fire. I need to land or we'll burn up."

"Listen up, chicken-yeller. If you try to land, I'll put a bullet in your brain. We're going to make one more pass, I'm going to drop one more grenade, and then you can land this bird. Not before."

T.F. had already banked the craft and came charging down the hill. The boy and the horse fled for the fold in the coulee. As the plane neared, the boy yanked left on the reins. A few seconds later, a grenade rolled ahead of the horse and exploded.

62

When the boy awoke, he lay flat on his back on a mound of prairie grass. The horse stood over him nibbling a cheek. Dazed, he sat up and checked his arms and legs. Everything appeared to be working. His ribs ached and some shrapnel had peppered a thigh, but he was alive. He guessed he had been unconscious for at least ten minutes. When he turned to his left, in the direction of the Beechcraft's last heading, a dark plume of smoke was drifting his direction. A distant explosion stirred the horse and he figured T.F. had waited too long to land and had crashed. He stood and brushed himself off, retrieved the canteen and rifle, and washed the caked blood off his cheek before taking a swig. He turned around to inspect the horse. Its chest oozed thick with blood, having taken the brunt of the explosion. The horse stood at attention eyeing him bug-eyed and spooked. The boy stroked the horse on the cheek. "I'm okay, Old Fella, but it looks like you're hurting somethin' bad." He took hold of the reins and walked the horse up the hill. For now, there was nothing he could do but let the horse continue to bleed. Soon, there would be others looking for him or the downed aircraft, and he had to keep moving. He led the horse up the hill, in the direction of Laurel and the Yellowstone River valley, and disappeared over the ridge.

When they reached the river, the sun lay low on the horizon. The river's current ran swift but the boy and the horse managed to swim across with the boy clinging to the horse's tail. The boy had hoped the river would wash away the blood coated on the horse's chest and that maybe the bloodletting had ceased. Once out of the water, however, the wounds gushed a fresh flow of red that ebbed down the horse's leg and to the sandbar they rested upon. The boy pressed his hands over the gaping holes but no amount of pressure could hold back the flow from so many porous wounds. He took out his hunting knife, cut his shirt into pieces, and stuffed the larger wounds with the cloth. In a matter of seconds, the cloth strips soaked through, passing even more blood. It was then the boy realized he could not stop the hemorrhaging and that his horse was dying. Still, he refused to abandon the horse to face death alone on the riverbank, so he led it onward, through the tall grass and toward the rail yard less than a hundred yards away.

In the distance, an empty boxcar's door spread open. The train rolled west and the boy knew this might be his only opportunity to escape. He dropped the reins, ran ahead, and pulled himself inside the car, just in time to watch Laurel disappear in the slow bend of the tracks following the course of the river. The events of the day proved too much and the boy buried his face in his hands and sobbed. He was leaving without his horse and without a proper sendoff. He remained sobbing for what seemed like minutes, ashamed over all he had done and over the abandonment of his horse, when a sound caught his attention. He glanced up. The horse was now galloping next to the boxcar and panting in gurgled spurts. It struggled to keep pace with the train and stumbled with each additional ounce of blood loss. The horse growled a low whicker and the boy hollered, "I'll never forget you, Old Fella." Suddenly, the horse tripped and collapsed to the ground in a tumbled heap. The boy watched the horse try to stand before re-collapsing and squealing in pain. The sight of the horse suffering caused the boy to leap out of the car and run back to where it lay. He fell to his knees and gathered the horse's head in his arms but the horse was already lapsing into unconsciousness.

"I'll see you in my Montana heaven," the boy kept saying over-and-over. "Wait for me there, Old Fella. Just wait for me there."

When dawn broke, the boy still lay with his horse. He had fallen asleep cradling it until it had passed away. What stirred the boy from slumber, however, was not the harsh sound of a siren but, rather, the gentle squeeze to the back of his neck. "Wake up, son," the voice whispered.

The boy blinked his eyes open and gazed up at the familiar face. "How'd you find me, Sheriff?" he asked.

"I monitored the airplane's radio. I knew everything. Just couldn't get to you before nightfall." The Sheriff looked at the white horse and let loose with a sad smile. "Sorry about your horse." He paused to study its familiar face. "You know," he said, "one good horse is all a man ever needs in a lifetime. Looks like you found yours."

LXIII

When I finished telling Annie my story I laid back down on the hospital bed. Talking nonstop tends to tire a body. Annie asked me if there was anything she could do to make me more comfortable and I said, "Yes," and pointed to the top drawer next to the bed. She opened the drawer and looked inside and nodded her head. She knew exactly what I wanted her to do.

"So, Billy," she says, "let me see if I understand all of this. You spent the next seventy years of your life here, behind this prison's walls, and willingly took the blame for killing all those men. Is that right?"

"Yes, far as taking the blame for the killings goes," I said. "No, far as spending the past seventy years in this prison. There was a spell when I broke out but the law caught up with me in Oregon. I had some unfinished business to attend to. Don't you know."

"But why didn't you tell the Sheriff that Lieutenant Mullin killed Sully and Bob?" she asked.

"What difference would it have made? I got four hundred years without parole for murder and attempted murder. Drop Sully and Bob and I still got two hundred. A man can only live so long, Annie. Eighty-seven is all I'm good for. Besides. No one woulda believed my story, anyways. It woulda been my word against Captain Belial's. Far as Sully and Bob. They know I didn't kill 'em. That's good by me."

"But nobody knows what really happened at Potrero Gap." She continued to press. "The newspapers had it all wrong."

"Heck. I believe I just told you, Annie." I smiled and winked at her. "You knowing the truth gives me piece of mind. But you

saving my Montana mustangs cuzza my story. . . now that's part of something far bigger."

Those were my last words. I remember wanting to say more. Heck. In the end we all wantta say more. But time had run out. . . .

I mentioned earlier how I had bad dreams about the things I did when I was seventeen. About how those bad dreams kept me awake at night. Gave me the ulcers and made me sick. I had a few good dreams too. One in particular I don't mind sharing. Goes like this:

It's at night. I'm alone. I'm lost in darkness. I see a light up ahead and follow it. It leads me to a man holding a lantern. He says to me, "It has been a long time, boy. What took you?"

And I say, "I was looking for the moon, Hayyel. Not your darned lantern."

He says back to me, "Sometimes the moon, it does not cooperate. You have to improvise."

"So, what do we do now, old friend?" I ask.

"You are so ignorant," he says. "We ride the wild horses. That is what we do. That is what we always do." He then points to the mountain. "See. Over there. Your white horse, Remliel, he waits for you. He is the one who told me to look for your spirit."

The next thing I know I'm riding my horse as fast as I can with my Pa and my Ma and Polly and old Duke cheering me on. I'm racing the ancient ones in an endless field of green clover. Polly she turns to everyone and says, "Look at Billy. He's winning. Ain't he grand." Hearing her voice again makes me happy. Hearing all their voices puts me at peace. That's when I lean forward and whisper in my horse's ear, "Do you hear all of 'em, Old Fella? Do you hear 'em cheering us on? You know what it means, don't you? It means we made it to my Montana heaven."

64

On a clear night, when the next full moon arrived, Annie drove to Potrero Gap and climbed Bopwadesh Hill. She hiked to the spot where the rare aspens grow and hung a mane of a white horse beneath one of the limbs. Then, she bowed her head in a moment of silence and when she finished, gazed up at the moon and whispered, "Pleasant dreams, Billy Bartell, wherever you are."

CPSIA information can be obtained at www.ICGtesting.com
234450LV00002B/69/P

9 781892 617163